THE SHAMAN'S PORTAL

The Shaman's Portal

GREGG STANDRIDGE

Forward

Thin places. Those places where other worlds rub against ours, wearing down the barrier between them. Places where what separates our world from the next is less like a wall, unyielding and impenetrable, and more like a curtain that can be pulled aside, allowing those who are attuned to such things a glimpse into other realms. Or, perhaps, more than a glimpse.

Cultures from the ancient Hindus to the Celts to Native Americans believed in the existence of these sacred spaces. The exact nature of these places varies depending on the people. Early Christians sought the divine in man-made structures like churches or sepulchers, while pagans usually found these sacred spaces in nature.

In ancient times, however, touching other worlds was more common. The boundaries between worlds seemed more porous then. Most people believed they were surrounded in their daily lives by gods and beings from other realms. The world they lived in was filled with spirits and sprites, some benign, some baleful. But as hunting/gathering gave way to an agrarian lifestyle, which gave way to an industrial one, which in turn has given way to our information-based, Internet-connected world, these spaces seem to be disappearing. Perhaps they've calcified from disuse, hardening such that what was once translucent has become opaque. Or maybe it's us; maybe the window is still open but we no longer choose to look through it.

It is within one of these remaining thin places where we first meet Ebrnt Tendigrads, or "Tendi" as he prefers to be known, a visitor — though an unintentional one — from a world similar to ours, albeit with some significant differences. In his world Tendi is a shaman, capable of controlling powerful magical forces via wands that he expertly crafts. Heralding the entrance of this extraordinary character into our world, he arrives in a blast of fire and fury, a literal Big Bang.

When I first met Gregg Standridge, Tendigrads' creator (and alter-ego), some forty years ago, it wasn't nearly as dramatic. No explosion, no green fire. And it wasn't in a thin place; it was a band house and Gregg had come over to audition. The house, while fun, didn't seem like a particularly special place, at least spiritually. Yet during that audition (which he nailed, of course) and through many rehearsals there, Gregg would seemingly commune with other worlds, conjuring magic. Unlike his alter-ego, he used a guitar rather than a wand, but the results were equally astonishing. Whereas Tendigrads traces magical sigils in the air, Gregg would weave beautiful, improvised melodic lines out of thin air. And he would go on to mesmerize audiences — as well as his bandmates — in gigs on stages throughout Oklahoma.

Gregg turned his hand to teaching music and, once again, seemed to have the magic touch. As someone who has studied with him off and on for the better part of thirty years, he has continued to astound me with a preternatural ability to explain and demonstrate simply and clearly concepts that had confused and eluded me for years. He has done this in his house, in apartments, in rooms in various teaching studios, none of which seemed to have an obvious mystical connection to other planes.

Yet no matter the location, Gregg could still seemingly draw on ethereal knowledge from another place.

As his restless mind turns to other pursuits, Gregg continues to enchant us, even without his ersatz wand. Whether through his line art, writing and staging a musical, his incredibly intricate woodworking and beautiful marquetry, or now with his first novella, Gregg seems to effortlessly commune with other worlds and channel their magic into this one. Though I've had the pleasure and awe of witnessing this in all its many forms for decades now, it still amazes me. I have seen him do this in many, many different places and spaces, yet surely they can't *all* be thin places. But maybe there's another secret to this. Maybe the secret is that Tendi — I mean Gregg — carries his thin place within himself, so that he can always reach through that portal and bring some magic into this world to delight us.

Brian Eads
Norman, Oklahoma
June 2025

Chapter One

Tommy Red Corn wondered where the tomatoes piled on the stainless steel table came from. "Probably Mexico," he thought out loud. He wondered why eighty-five percent of the produce he cut at Maxine's Fine Dining came from Mexico. It just seemed kind of odd that you could live in Oklahoma, where there was plenty of room to grow stuff, and yet it all seemed to come from Mexico. Tommy was a slim built young man of 19 years. His white soda jerk hat was trying desperately to contain his coarse black hair and a threadbare polyester necktie gathered the collar of his white short sleeve dress shirt with a sloppily done half-Windsor knot as the tail stubbornly twisted over the front.

Tommy had worked at Maxine's for over two years now. He had gone full-time after dropping out of high school in his junior year, and for Tommy, it really wasn't that hard of a choice. His parents were not here to tell him to finish and basketball, the only slight joy he got out of school, was pretty much off the shelf when he lost his starting position to some hot shot senior who moved to town from Tulsa. There were also his grades, which were marginal at best. It was pretty much impossible to work enough hours to pay rent and utilities and study, so he did what in his mind was the logical thing.

He set to work washing the tomatoes and cutting them into wedges for the salads, his serrated knife flying faster than was probably safe. When he finished, he flipped the knife up in the air, watched it do a 360, and caught it perfectly by the white nylon handle. He winked at Helen Easton, the salad maker who was leading his station tonight.

"Better not let Mr. Carr catch you playing around, boy! He's in a mood tonight!" muttered Helen. Mr. Carr came out as "Mistah Caaaw" with her heavy Boston accent.

Tommy nodded at her with the slightest of grins and looked at Helen's handiwork, an amazing Waldorf salad that was one of the trademarks of Maxine's. Helen had worked here for almost twenty years, and she had always been kind to Tommy, almost like a mom in many ways.

"So what's got him all fired up, Helen?" Tommy asked.

"That new girl didn't show up for her shift," she said in a lowered voice, "and the only one he could get to cover it was Anson."

Tommy cringed at that. Since kindergarten, Anson had been his best friend, but the thought of him waiting tables on a Saturday night at Maxine's was frightening at best. He knew he would be helping his buddy out tonight after his prep shift was up.

Surprisingly, Anson did fairly well that night. He almost dropped a tray but managed to keep it from spilling all over the kitchen floor. He also caught a break with a generous tip from a group of blue-haired ladies who had probably drunk too much wine and thought he was handsome.

Tommy teased Anson about them. "So, which one will you take to the prom, ATV?" Anson's nickname was from his initials, Anson Thomas Vernon.

"Chill on that crap, Tommy. They were nice ladies. Just a little drunk is all," Anson replied."

"Well, don't let them keep you out too late at the Bingo Hall!" Tommy chided.

"Dude! Knock it off already! Hey, did you hear what happened to Talula?" Anson asked.

"Well, I heard she missed her shift. Was she out looking for ancient artifacts again? Or maybe she was investigating 'paranormal activity' and just lost track of time," Tommy observed with a smirk on his face. "That girl is pretty, but man, she is weird!"

"No, man. Way crazier than that. She went out to the Shaman's Portal and was doing some exploring, and something blew up out there. It scorched her hair and burned her face. I'm going to the hospital as soon as we close. You coming?"

Tommy considered it for a moment. He was pretty beat, but he was off tomorrow, so he agreed to go see Talula. He wondered how badly she was burned and was also more than curious about the explosion.

"Sure, I'll go. I hope she is okay."

Everyone in the Oklahoma Panhandle knows the legends surrounding the Shaman's Portal. Spanish explorer Francisco Vázquez de Coronado traveled through the region in the 1500s in search of gold. Native Americans tried to warn him of the perils of the dunes, but Coronado didn't listen. Three of his men disappeared without a trace into flashes of green light while exploring the area. There have been other accounts of people who have simply vanished – some say into an alternate dimension – in the same way. Of course, nobody really believes that stuff around Beaver, Oklahoma. But Tommy and Anson were just a little creeped out when they saw Talula in the hospital bed. Her face was bandaged, and her arm was in a sling. She was lying very still, and the boys immediately thought the worst when they saw her in this condition.

But then she opened her eyes and squealed in surprise. "Oh my God! I am so glad you guys came!" She sat up in bed quite comfortably as if she had no injuries. She swung her legs out to the edge of the bed and hopped onto the floor. "You are not going to believe what I saw at the Shaman's Portal!" she exclaimed as she waved her good hand in the air and began to pace the floor.

"Uh, Talula, are you okay? I mean, you look like hell...your uh, face. I mean, all those bandages?" Anson stuttered.

"Yeah, maybe you should get back in bed?" Tommy added.

"I am fine!" Talula exclaimed. I have first-degree burns, is all, like a weak sunburn. My arm is sprained, but I'll be okay. The only reason they are keeping me is that they think I hit my head."

"Well, that's good, I guess," Tommy said.

"Yeah, cool. So when are they going to release you?" Anson asked.

"I get out tomorrow, as long as my head checks out. But you will not believe what I saw in the sand dunes!" Talula blurted.

At just that moment, a nurse came in and yelled at the boys. "You two! Out now! It's 30 minutes past visiting hours! And you, Miss Trouble! Get back in bed, pronto!"

"But, I need to..." Talula protested.

"Out now! In bed NOW!" The nurse commanded.

The boys rushed out of the room without hearing Talula's story.

"I'll tell you tomorrow," she said as the nurse chased the boys out into the hallway.

Tommy and Anson left the hospital, walking west on Calhoon Blvd. towards their garage apartment on East 9th. Beaver is a tiny little town with fewer than fifteen hundred people. It is the seat of Beaver County, so it could be said that it is the cultural center of the Oklahoma Panhandle. But the dirty sky and the dust-driving winds are enough to remind you where you are in No Man's Land. The boys leaned into the hot, dry wind. It was almost ten o'clock at night, but in July, it was still in the nineties, with temperatures reaching well into the triple digits during the heat of the day.

"Well, she sounds okay to me," Tommy finally offered. "I mean, it looked pretty bad with all those bandages on her face, but she'll be fine."

"Yeah, you're probably right," Anson agreed, "but that was pretty scary, Tommy."

It was obvious to Tommy that Anson had feelings for Miss Talula Polk. They had been friends since kindergarten, and they were even boyfriend/girlfriend for a short time in the fourth grade. But like many grade school romances, they broke up.

Talula was very smart, and her family was much better off than Anson's. So when they graduated high school, Anson tried a year of a technical school in nearby Liberal, Kansas, hoping to get an Automotive Technician's Certificate in two years. But he soon found out that the gas money driving his '68 Plymouth Roadrunner to and from Liberal five days a week quickly drained his meager savings. He quit after one semester.

Talula had the grades to be admitted to several schools. But she chose Panhandle State, which was fairly close to home and offered her a full ride to study chemistry. Even though she really loved archaeology and Native American history, her father convinced her that making a living in those fields would be difficult.

"But chemistry!" Her father exclaimed. "Oil companies are always hiring chemists!"

So she did as her father suggested and enrolled at Panhandle State to study Chemistry. Anson was pretty excited when Talula showed up on his doorstep at the beginning of summer to hang out. He quickly helped her get a job waiting tables at Maxine's.

Tommy couldn't help but see the change in Anson's demeanor when Talula came home. There was just a tinge of annoyance that surfaced when Anson would try to slip off and hang with Talula without him. But it wasn't all that bad. Talula was a unique, interesting girl, and there was always some sort of excitement whenever she was around. Excitement was in short supply in Beaver, Oklahoma.

Neither boy said a word until they turned onto Quinn Avenue.

"Whaddya think she was doing out there?" Tommy wondered out loud. No response. "Are you sleepwalking, ATV?"

Anson swerved into Tommy, feigning a sleepwalking zombie. They had a short laugh.

"We drove out to those Indian ruins on the Mason's ranch, and she found something out there," Anson said in a more serious tone.

"What was it?"

"Well, I thought it was just a weird-shaped rock, but now I am beginning to wonder. It looked like an octopus made out of flint, and she was losing her mind when she found it. She said it looked similar to a design she had seen at the Shaman's Portal. I think she took that octorock thing out there and made something happen!"

"Like what?" Tommy said as he stepped into the street and turned to Anson.

"Hell, I don't know, Tommy. That place has some weird juju. Always has. I think she might have messed with something she shouldn't have. What if she opened up the portal somehow?" Anson was getting wound up.

"Come on, Anson, that's just tourist trap stuff. There's no portal out there! I don't know what she did, but I bet you it had to do with her chemistry set or something like that."

"I'm telling you, Tommy, this has got nothing to do with a chemistry set! She may be in trouble, and we need to watch out for her." Anson was wild now. His arms were flying all over the place, and he was pacing back and forth on the street in front of their apartment.

"Okay, man, chill. We'll see her in the morning. It's Sunday, so no work. We will get to the bottom of it. Look, we saw her, and she was fine.

Anson calmed down a little as Tommy put an arm around his shoulder. "We'll go check on her first thing tomorrow. Promise."

Anson slumped in resignation, realizing that there was little he could do tonight.

"Come on." Tommy said, "We still got a few beers in the fridge. Let's cool out and watch MASH."

"Killer," Anson muttered halfheartedly.

"I wonder how long Klinger's going to wear those dresses."

Chapter Two

Helen Easton rose before sunrise like she had almost every day of her life. Her old bones creaked nowadays as she made a cup of Sanka instant coffee, decaf. She pulled a Virginia Slim cigarette out of the pack and lit it with a book of matches lying on the table. She looked at the print on the side of the pack that read *The Surgeon General has determined that cigarette smoking is dangerous to your health.*

"More dangerous for people around me if I tried to quit," she muttered.

Sitting in her kitchen chair, she stared out the window at the garage apartment she rented to Tommy and Anson. She wondered about those two boys. Helen had watched both of them grow up when Tommy lived across the street. She knew Tommy's parents before the accident that claimed his dad's life, and eventually, his Mother's life, too. Tommy's dad, Toby, had been a good soul. He worked hard, coached Little League baseball and basketball, and worked in the oilfield. He was an excellent high school basketball player, and he led the Dusters to the quarter-finals of the state championship in his senior year. Tommy's mom, Rosa, was Toby's high-school sweetheart, and they married straight after graduating. Rosa had worked at Maxine's with Helen for many years.

One night, the two had been out at a bar. On the return trip home, Toby slammed into a stranded car in the middle of the road. Toby died instantly, and Rosa was critically injured. Rosa blamed herself as the two were arguing when the accident happened. Tommy was 13 at the time. Rumors swirled that Toby was drunk, which caused the accident, even though his blood-alcohol level was under the required level.

Rosa had a long, difficult recovery, and although she could eventually walk, she needed crutches to get anywhere. And then there was the pain. She was always in terrible pain, both physically and emotionally, so she took more pain pills. She couldn't work; she eventually lost the house and ended up moving in with a cousin. Only three months after moving, she was found unconscious due to an overdose of pain pills. At sixteen years old, Tommy Redcorn lost his mother.

Helen remembered the funerals. Toby's funeral was just heartbreaking, and Tommy was inconsolable. But Rosa's was lightly attended, and Tommy was stone-faced through it all. Tommy drifted between Helen's home and Anson's home that first year and eventually saved up enough money from working to get a little apartment. But it was clear he couldn't pay the bills and go to school. He was evicted after six months and was back surfing couches. Helen stepped in and made him a deal on the old garage apartment. If Tommy fixed it up, Helen would let him stay there for free for the first year, and then Tommy could start paying rent. That worked out great for everyone concerned, and when Anson moved in with Tommy and shared rent, it was even better. The two boys helped her with things around the house, and she really enjoyed having them around. She didn't know where they would land, but they seemed to have found their footing for now.

Helen snuffed out her cigarette, finished dressing, and waited for her friend, Jane, to pick her up for church.

Chapter Three

The little converted garage apartment wasn't much, but it was clean. The one-bedroom was basically a loft where you couldn't stand up to full height. The lower part was an open living/kitchen area with a small bathroom and shower in the corner with a flowered plastic curtain. There was one small, exposed "closet." The kitchen cabinets were made out of white-painted plywood, while the countertops had new, horrible avocado green Formica, someone's idea of modern and cheap. The water tank was exposed next to the tiny gas range. Still, the boys were proud to have the place.

Anson woke up Tommy at eight o'clock, raring to see Talula. "Come on, man! Let's roll out!"

Tommy slid down the ladder and went straight to the bathroom while Anson poured some Wheaties into a couple of bowls and started the coffee percolating.

Anson poured a cup and set it on the bathroom counter for Tommy. "Mucho gracias," Tommy replied as he took a swig and climbed into the shower.

After wolfing down the cereal, the boys got dressed and drove to the hospital, feeling the heat of the day already coming on. Visiting hours had just begun when they got to the hospital, so they went straight to Talula's room.

She was there waiting for them, practically jumping up and down with excitement. Her bandages had been removed, and her cheeks looked a bit red, but other than that, her face seemed totally fine. Her hair, on the other hand, had been badly singed, especially on the right side of her face.

"Hey, Talula! What's the buzz?" The boys greeted her.

She jumped out of the bed and gave Anson a quick hug. "Finally! I haven't slept thinking about what happened; you are not going to believe it!" she said.

Anson, who was still recovering from the shock of the unexpected hug, had no reply.

"Spill the beans then," Tommy urged. They all sat on the bed, Talula's legs dangling, while the boy's long legs toed the off-white tile.

"Well, I made a huge discovery on the Mason ranch," she began. "Remember that little stone circle I told you guys about? Well, I dug down a little way and found this amazing flint stone shaped like an octopod. It's a little smaller than my hand, and I remembered seeing the same shape indented in the rocks by the Shaman's portal!"

Tommy nodded as he listened, not really remembering anything about the little stone circle or any of that stuff.

"This is where it really gets crazy," she continued. "I took the stone out to the portal and found that indentation that I remembered. They matched! Then I placed the octopod rock in, and all of a sudden, green lights started flashing. It suddenly turned dark like night, but with that amazing green light tracing all over the sky. Then BOOM! Big explosion! It almost knocked me out! I was dazed and realized that my face was burned. My glasses were smoked, and my shirt and jeans were even a bit charred."

At all of this, Tommy began to show a little skepticism. If her clothes were burnt, it stood to reason that her arms and legs would be burnt as well.

"And this is the absolutely unbelievable part!" She went on. "This old man appeared out of thin air, with very long gray hair and a huge beard, wearing a buckskin robe. I screamed; the burns hurt so badly! He walked over to me, scooped me up in his arms, and laid me on the edge of a large flat rock. He was talking in some native language at first, but quickly switched to English. He told me to lie still and that he would help me. I was in a lot of pain; my face was on fire, and my arms and legs were hurting, too. He held a stick, like a magic wand, muttered something, traced a pattern in the air with the stick, and pointed the wand at me. Then I felt this coolness flow over me and fell asleep immediately. I don't know how long I was out, but it couldn't have been too long. I woke up feeling like my face was a little bit sore, but nothing like it was. And the old man was gone."

Tommy and Anson stared at each other with wide eyes; neither knew what to say after such a wild story. Anson offered the first question. "Talula, did you maybe...when your head hit something ,uh..."

Talula was having none of that. "I know what I saw, Anson!" she stated defiantly. "It was as real as you and I are standing here. That old man saved my life, or at least kept me from being disfigured."

Tommy was less diplomatic. "Come on, Talula! You just hit your head and had some weird dream. There's no way all that stuff actually happened!"

Talula folded her hands across her lap and stared intently at Tommy.

"Well, it is true that I may have hit my head, but it is also true that I was burned really badly. And my skin looks like it has been healing for a couple of weeks now, instead of 18 hours," she said. "This morning I heard the doctors talking about how fast I'm healing; they can't explain it either. I know what I saw, Tommy Red Corn."

Tommy dropped his head and stared at the white linoleum. He really didn't know what to believe. He did know that Talula wanted to believe in all kinds of hoodoo. But she had never gone off the deep end like this. She always tried to be pretty scientific about any sort of ghost stories or unexplained mysteries she encountered. And she usually had some explanation that would pull the curtain back on most of those stories.

Anson spoke up. "I believe you, Ta," he assured her while awkwardly patting her on the shoulder. "I'm just so glad you're all right! Hey, what has your dad said about it?"

"I haven't told him yet. He's busy in Tucson doing some consulting work," she said. "I want to check out a few things first, and if he knows about this, he will be home faster than a speeding bullet. I don't want this to get out at all, if possible."

She jumped down off the bed and went into the bathroom, taking her street clothes with her. She started changing with the door cracked open so she could talk. "First thing we are going to do is to go out there and look around. I need to see if that octopod is still there. And we need to see if we can find that old man.

"We?" Tommy said. "I don't feel like going out to the sand dunes on my only day off. And I bet the doctors aren't going to want you crawling around out there today. It's like 102 in the shade!"

"Come on, Tommy! We can't let her go alone! There might be some crazy old man out there, or...it could be anything! I'll go with you, Ta." Anson said.

Tommy gave Anson a major stink eye.

Anson was one who tended to want to believe all the mystic hoo-hah, too. He swore he saw flying saucers, and he ate up all the Shaman's Portal stories, so it made sense that he was trying to persuade Tommy to go.

"Come on, Red Corn!" said Talula. "Tell you what. If you go with us, I'll buy dinner tonight. How about KFC? All you can eat!"

Talula grinned at him with big brown eyes, flashing a look that said, 'I gotcha on that one.'

Tommy looked around and thought about it for a few seconds. "They haven't even released you yet. So I guess we can't go anyways."

As if on cue, the nurse walked in with Talula's release papers. Talula walked out of the bathroom in her dirty jeans, a sleeved baseball shirt that announced she was a Disco Queen, and a St Louis Cardinals baseball cap. She listened closely to the nurse's instructions, signed the papers, which included no driving until checking in with her family doctor, and assured the nurse that Anson was there to pick her up and take her straight home.

When the nurse left, Talula turned to the boys and said, "Let's book!" She moved out the door with Anson on her heels. Tommy muttered something under his breath and shuffled off after them. The only good thing coming out of this would be the fried chicken, he thought, as he chased down his two friends.

Chapter Four

The old man named Tendigrads, hidden by his magic from all but the most discerning eye, sat quietly on a rock. He had also managed to adjust the air around him, so it wasn't so hot. But his magic was not going to get him out of his current predicament. He pondered his situation and wondered how he came to fall into the portal that brought him to this land. It smelled so strange, and the land was so barren. Obviously, he was somewhere else, but there was something familiar about this land, nonetheless. And the girl. A girl of the first people, but she was dressed so strangely, some sort of royalty by the words on her tunic. He had almost killed her with his spell.

He had the misfortune of having been ambushed by a kigatilik, a violent demon, especially known for hunting shaman and wizards. The old wizard had cast a fireball just as he saw the green lights swallow up the kigatilik. He was then in a new world where his spell discharged close to the young girl, burning her badly and fracturing her arm. The girl was screaming in pain, and so he immediately healed her of the most serious injuries, but now he wondered what the repercussions would be. She had seen him.

He deduced that he had walked right into an ancient portal between this world and his. The kigatilik had not followed, and so he assumed the portal was closed. He paced back and forth over the area where he first appeared, but found nothing that would trigger the portal to open again. He was at a loss and regretted letting the girl see him. He also wished he had gotten some information from her before she left.

His belly rumbled, and he reached in his bag for a strip of jerky and some corn dodgers. He had a skin of water, but because he appeared to be in a desert, he decided to hold off drinking until he could find more water. He decided he would wait another day. Maybe the portal would trigger open at the same time tomorrow. If that didn't work, well, he would have to enlist the aid of this world's shaman. For now, however, sleep seemed like a good plan. As he lay on his back, he could see the Seven Sisters and the Big Dipper in the night sky. So he knew he was in the same land as his, but in a different...when or where? Or maybe a different time or place? It was very confusing, and even though he was well-versed in mysticism, he had no experience with alternate realities.

His old muscles finally started to relax, and his mind calmed as his eyes finally began to close. He dreamed of his home in Tahlequah and of his workshop where he made wands and staffs. He dreamed of the young men and women coming to his workshop to have him craft a wand for them. He also dreamed of his childhood in the new land of the firstborn and how the Shaman passed him over because of the blood of his mother. All these things slowly spun in Tendigrads' mind as he drifted in and out of sleep.

And that is how the legendary wand maker from The Territory of The First People spent his first night in this strange new land.

Chapter Five

1850 in Tendigrads' world

Some tribes say the fall was simply a natural occurrence. That the earth is in constant flux and that the layers of our Mother shifted in such a way that the Eastern and Western seaboards experienced massive earthquakes and tidal waves, leaving what we know in our reality as Southern and Western prairies to be the most inhabitable lands of North America. Others point to the Great Octopod that sleeps at the bottom of the ocean. The creature was so large that three of its tentacles were in the Great Eastern Ocean, while the other five were in the Great Western Ocean. These tribes believe that the Great Octopod adjusted itself during his eternal sleep and caused the massive disaster.

The lands mainly thought of as the Lands of the White Settlers were no more. Almost everything east of the Mississippi River was underwater. The lands that we know as Mississippi, Missouri, and Louisiana became unimaginable swampland where massive reptilian beasts roamed. All of California and half of Nevada fell into the sea. Much of Mexico also fell. The lands to the north were fairly intact, but the United States was no longer. Those who had been pushed out of their homes and relocated to the center of America had mostly avoided the tragic end that befell most of the European Americans.

The land began to see monsters and magical creatures from the old legends of native lore. And the First People found that they were touched by magic, a very tangible magic that varied in power throughout the folk. They found they could influence weather, cre-

ate fire, heal the sick and wounded, and even repel the monstrosities that sometimes attacked their towns and villages.

And so a new life began for The First People. They began to study magic and mysticism, sorcery, and abjuration. Tendigrads, being half Cherokee, was one of the few non-pure-blood natives to have the gift. But when the Shaman came to Tahlequah, he did not choose Tendigrads to study with the others, so Tendigrads was forced to study on his own. One of the most amazing things he discovered was the way that wood and other natural materials conducted magic and how different woods and gemstones could greatly strengthen or diminish the effects of a spell.

The Shaman eventually discovered that the work Tendigrads was doing was of great value. This became a huge advance in the magical community. Soon, Tendigrads was sharing his knowledge with others who had the gift to create with wood. He was also the primary choice to make the wands and staffs of new magic students. Although his magic skills weren't as powerful or refined as the brightest who studied with the great shaman of the land, he was highly revered for his advances in wand making.

Chapter Six

Talula, Anson, and Tommy piled into the metallic blue Roadrunner and headed out State Highway 23 to the sand dunes. Anson was pressing the Plymouth with Talula sitting between him and Tommy, his foot a bit heavy on the accelerator.

"In a hurry, ATV?" Tommy inquired.

Anson backed off the gas a touch. "Naw, just trying to get some air moving in here."

Tommy nodded. There was no air conditioning in the Roadrunner. Talula wasn't saying anything, but Tommy could almost see her mental gears grinding as they pulled onto the road that led to the sand dunes.

"I wonder who he is?" she finally asked out loud. "And I wonder where he came from."

Tommy resisted the urge to snicker. But he was hoping that they could prove to Talula that this was just some *I-got-hit-in-the-head-and-lost-my-mind-for-a-while* thing and they would soon be done with it.

"Maybe he is from the past," Anson offered. "I mean the whole mountain man, buckskin thing and all, it would seem that would be the most likely answer."

"Yeah, but the magical spell and the wand or scepter, or whatever it was, maybe it's not a past thing at all. Maybe it's an alternate reality thing," Talula replied.

This time Tommy snorted; he couldn't catch himself. Talula looked at him as if he had just shot her dog. He quickly looked out the window. "Here we are," he said. "Where did you see him, Talula?" Tommy was really trying hard not to aggravate his friends with logic, but it was kind of difficult when they were deep off in *Twilight Zone* mode.

"It's up about a quarter mile on the right," Talula said, seeming to forget about Tommy's slight indiscretion. Anson parked the car where she had pointed, and they hopped out.

The sand dunes really brought the heat down on them. Anson grabbed the canteen of water he had filled up at the hospital, and they trudged off into the sand. Talula led the way and began sprinting straight to the spot of her encounter with the old man. She shuffled through the rock and sand dislodged by the explosion, looking for any sign of the stone octopod. But even the small rock footing where the impression had stood for so many years was gone.

"What are you looking for, Ta?" Anson asked as he and Tommy jogged up to the site.

"I was hoping to find the key, but it appears to have been blown to smithereens."

"What key?" Tommy asked.

"The octopus-looking rock," Anson injected, trying to diffuse any more bickering between his friends.

He could see Talula was getting more frustrated as she dug frantically in the sand.

"Let's look and see if we can find any signs of the old man," she said, as she moved off to the trail a little further from the explosion site.

"It does look like something blew up here," Tommy said, with just a hint of wonder. Anson continued to dig in the dirt half-heartedly, as Tommy tried to decide what caused this damage. He was definitely not on board with the whole Gandalf of the Wild West idea, but he sensed that there was something strange going on. Talula came back looking dejected.

"Well, there is no sign of him here," she said. "I can't believe that the key and pedestal were destroyed. That really sucks!" she muttered, sitting down on the edge of a freshly exposed layer of rocks.

"I don't know what happened here, Ta, but I can see that something did blow up," Tommy acknowledged, "I don't know how you survived it."

"I already told you; that old man saved me," she insisted. "If he hadn't appeared, I would have probably died out here." Anson was still shuffling around in the dirt with his shoe.

"Well, what's next, then?" he said.

"What do you say we get out of this heat? Get back and hit the KFC? I mean, I was promised chicken," Tommy proclaimed, trying to lighten the mood. "Come on, Talula. Let's get back to town, and we can talk about it over a bucket of Colonel Sander's finest."

"Alright, alright...Let's go. We better feed Red Corn as promised," she said, showing just a hint of a smile.

Anson kicked a couple of small sticks out of the hole he was scratching in the ground and sent them flying towards the trail. "Nice boot there, ATV," Talula said, as the tiny sticks landed an impressive thirty feet down the trail.

"Yeah! Impressive!" added Tommy. The three friends headed back to the powder blue Plymouth.

As they piled into the steaming hot car, the two little sticks that Anson had so casually booted across the sand began to roll in the wind along the dune. But then they actually moved together and joined each other side by side. Next, three others emerged from the sand and slowly joined together to form the rotten remains of a gnarled, skeletal hand that began to slowly crawl out towards the road.

Chapter Seven

Tendigrads woke early and began to scout the area in the morning light. After inspecting where he hoped the portal would be, his deep concern about returning to his own land increased. His fireball had damaged so much of the earth. He couldn't see any sort of altar or physical archway that might have held some clues. And so he sat out along the trail, his staff and meager belongings thrown over his shoulder in a knapsack.

He was ever reminded of the heat of this land. Even with the sun still rising, it was so much hotter than his own land. He was tempted to spend some of his magical energy to cool the air around him, but he had no idea what awaited him in this strange world, so he plodded on through the heat. His battered buckskin hat kept him shaded, but it was soon soaked with sweat, and his moccasin boots were hot and damp. Tendigrads finally came across a grey rock trail that was as smooth as pottery, and he sat for a moment trying to decipher which way to travel. As he meditated on his next move, a strange red wagon with unusual wheels and unbelievable amounts of silver decorating the sides sped past him. The wagon had no horses and appeared to be steam-powered, like a locomotive. But it was so fast! It was gone just as fast as it had appeared!

"Well, that must be the way, then," he muttered to himself. He stood up, stretched his tall, wiry frame, and began to head south along the strange path.

He soon found out that walking on the path was not the thing to do, as it seemed to drink the heat from the sun, so he kept to the side, occasionally exploring the land and returning to the side of the path at random intervals. He was taking a break in the shade of a scraggly bush when he heard another wagon coming up the path. This one was going north, and it was much louder than the other one. He caught a glimpse of a blue flash on the path as it seemed to fly out of his vision, and he wondered how the people of this land lived with such annoying sounds.

After his rest, he started back along the path as the sun crawled higher in the sky. He studied the sparse vegetation and small life that could be found skittering from rock to rock: horny toads, boomers, and such. He saw hawks, which was somewhat reassuring, and other birds common to his native lands. But the harshness of this land was overwhelming. In his land, there was still tall prairie grass full of life, even in the peak of the summer months. He saw no sign of bison here; he did see a few coyote and rabbit droppings, but that was it. After the sun had reached its peak, he heard the awful noise again. He turned to look behind him and saw the blue wagon racing down the path.

There was a heated discussion going on in the Roadrunner. The disco queen was on her pedestal preaching, and the two boys were having none of it. "If you can't dig KC and The Sunshine Band, then you really have no musical taste!" Talula yelled as she threw her hands up in the air.

"I could dance all night to that!"

"Har! They don't hold a candle to Skynyrd! Tommy shot back. "That is the most killer band around!"

"And Boston," Anson added. "Hey, 'More Than a Feeling' is a killer song! I can't wait till I get my 8-track fixed in this thing so we can listen to music stead of talking about it."

"There he is!! He's right there!" Talula screamed. "Pull over!" They all saw the buck-skinned clad figure as they topped the little rise in the road. Anson slammed on the brakes and skidded to a halt, leaving black marks in the road and dust swirling in the air as he slid off to the side.

Talula was out of the car instantly and ran back towards the strange old man. Tommy was right behind and yelled at Talula to slow down. He had no idea who this old guy was, but he was more than a little worried. Anson was close behind, but Talula arrived in front of the old man in a flash.

"Osiyo," Tendigrads offered to the young Queen with a slight bow.

"Uh... Hi, do you speak English? Talula asked. The boys followed quickly and heard the old man speaking.

"I can speak in English if you prefer, young Queen. I am familiar with many of the native languages. I see your wounds have healed. I am so grateful," he said. "I would also like to offer my apologies to you. It appears that my spell was cast right as I entered a portal from my world to this one. A kigatilik attacked me, and that was the target of my spell. Once again, I am so glad I was able to heal you."

The boys stared in disbelief as the old man told the story. He stood looking calmly at the three, leaning against his wooden staff, waiting for a response.

"Holy shit! Tommy finally said.

"I told you, but y'all wouldn't believe me," Talula said. "And here he is!" She gestured toward the old man. "Mister uh..."

"Master Tendigrads, my Queen. I am at your service!" The wizard stated as he bowed to Talula once again.

"I'm Talula, this is Anson, and that's Tommy Red Corn."

"Red Corn," exclaimed Tendigrads, "A young man of the Osage First People! It is an honor!"

"Yeah, nice to meet you," Tommy murmured back.

"Anson. This is an old English name, if I recall. Peace be with you, Son of England."

Anson was speechless.

"And Queen Talula! Running Waters! I am honored to be in the presence of the Queen of the Cherokee. I myself am Cherokee and Irish."

"I am not a queen, Master Tendigrads. I am just a girl with a little Cherokee blood and a Cherokee name."

"Oh, from your garment, I assumed you were a queen of some sort."

Talula looked down at her *DISCO QUEEN* shirt and laughed.

"That is truly a relief," Tendigrads said. "The idea of kings and queens in my native land tend to have a rather negative connotation. So I wonder if you and your young friends might lend me your assistance. I need to find a way back through the portal. To my own world. Where might I find a wizard or shaman who is versed in planar travel?"

The three looked at each other for a moment, and finally, Talula spoke up. "I don't know who could help. The idea of traveling through portals and planes is considered impossible," she said. "Not only that but when people start talking about such ideas, they are looked upon as crazy. But I do know what happened, or at least what I think happened."

Talula told her story of the octopod discovery and how she had placed it in the receptacle in the stone pedestal. She told how a mere second later, she felt the explosion.

"And that's when I came to be in this world," Tendigrads finished.

"Well, yes," Talula acknowledged.

"And do you still have the octopod?" Tendigrads asked.

"We looked for it but couldn't find it. I'm afraid it was shattered in the explosion. Even the pedestal with the receptacle was destroyed."

Tendigrads' head dropped at this news. "Well, I will have to seek lodging and supplies and think about this predicament.

There must be someone in your world who might be able to assist me."

"We will help you in any way possible. We can take you into town and get some food and talk more about what can be done," Talula said, taking the old man's arm and leading him to the car. Tommy and Anson were still trying to absorb what had just happened. As for Tommy, he was absolutely convinced that Talula's story was induced by the knock on the head she received during the explosion. But when her magic-wielding phantom was actually walking down 270 in full buckskin, with a wooden staff, he slowly began to realize that Talula was telling the truth.

"Let's go, man." Anson urged, and they headed to the car.

Chapter Eight

Questions were flying back and forth between Talula and Tendigrads. Sometimes Anson and Tommy would fill in the gaps. Still, the two people whose fates were linked at the Shaman's Portal were drinking in each other's information – how a car works, the power of magic, the evil creature that was chasing the wizard, and the value of disco in the world of music – faster than the boys could keep up with.

Tendigrads was amazed at the speed of the "roadrunner" and in a matter of minutes, they were pulling into Beaver.

"Go to your place first, Anson. We need to get him some clothes. He's about your size." Talula said.

"Cool." Anson nodded.

Tendigrads took in the surroundings as they drove past the buildings on the hard black road. He remembered going through St Louis and the buildings there, but this was amazing. The colors and stonework were just spectacular.

"What a beautiful village," he said with amazement.

The kids chuckled at that. "Wait till you see Tulsa or Oklahoma City," Tommy said.

"Oklahoma!" Tendigrads exclaimed, "In the Choctaw tongue, Oklahoma means red people! Perhaps I should travel to Oklahoma City. The first people may be my only chance to get back to my land."

"You won't find that many more Indians in Oklahoma City. Maybe you should try Durant, Tahlequah, Anadarko, those are the places you'll find Indians," Tommy suggested.

Tendigrads' eyes shone with a bit of discomfort at the word "Indians," but at the mention of Tahlequah, he became extremely excited.

"Tahlequah! That is where I'm from! In my world, that is. Maybe I can find a shaman or wizard there."

Talula interjected. "Your world seems to be one of magic, but the Indians in this world do not have that type of power."

Tendigrads frowned finally and questioned the young Cherokee woman. "That is a curious name for The First People! Indians! In my world, that name was an insult," the wizard said. "And you two, being of First People's blood, shouldn't use that word to describe yourselves or your race."

The three young people didn't comment, but it was definitely food for thought. Anson and Tommy dug through clothing at their apartment to find the wizard some suitable clothing. They pointed him to the shower because, well, he stank like an old man who had been wandering around in the wilds for a couple of weeks. Tendigrads commented on all the wonders. The shower, the television, the electrical appliances.

"Your world is well-versed in magic it would seem," he said. "With all of these amazing wonders, I am sure I will find a magician to help me get home."

Tommy had some old cowboy boots that were only a little loose, and Anson reluctantly gave up a brand new pair of Levi's that were a bit tight but fit well enough. Tommy came up with some socks, a belt, and underwear for the old man.

"Wait! One more thing!" Anson said. He pulled out a battered John Deere hat and put it on Tendigrads' head. They pointed to the mirror so the wizard could see his transformation.

"The peculiarities of your clothing are intriguing," Tendigrads stated. "What does this headdress mean? It appears to be a deer clan symbol, which is my clan. But who is John?"

"John Deere is a tractor company, like powered mules for farming," Anson said.

"Ahh, so what of horses and mules? I did notice some cattle when we were coming to town. Do these mechanical mules do all agriculture work?"

"Pretty much," Tommy said, "I guess there are some really poor people in the world that may still plow with mules. But no one I know."

"Hmmm, what a strange world," Tendigrads muttered.

Then Talula knocked on the door. "Hey! Can I come in now?"

Anson opened the door and swept his arm out in a grand entrance gesture with his big goofy smile.

"A pox upon me, my Disco Queen!" he quipped in a decent English accent.

Talula blushed as her eyes caught Anson's. "Okay, I guess I will have to get rid of my favorite shirt," she shot back.

She squeezed her way past the coffee table to where Tendigrads stood. She looked him up and down, told him to turn around, and pronounced him dressed just fine.

"Now we are going to need a cover story," she said. "Since you really are from Tahlequah, we will keep that the same. Let's say you are a history teacher at Northwestern State Teacher's College. You teach history with an emphasis on Cherokee history. You're Tommy's great uncle from his mom's side. How does that sound?"

They all looked at her with a touch of awe. "Dang Talula, you sound like you've been moonlighting for the CIA," Tommy exclaimed. "Why is he supposed to be related to me?"

"Because he will need to stay with you and Anson, so you can start calling him uncle... uh, we don't even know your first name, Master Tendigrads."

"Ebrnt," Tendigrads answered. "The cover story as you call it seems to be simple enough. I am sure there will be some need for improvisation. I will follow your lead, young friends. And there is no need to worry about me. I can sleep outside under the stars."

"No way, you can have the couch," Anson interjected. "It's best to stay inside at night. I don't think we want the police asking questions about you sleeping outside late at night."

"Yeah, we will make it work," Tommy added. "Now I need my KFC, so let's go. All we can eat, right Talula?"

"Yeah, that's what I said." Talula rolled her eyes.

"I hope you brought your piggy bank because I am hungry!"

And the four of them piled into Anson's Roadrunner.

Chapter Nine

The aroma of food in the KFC was overwhelming. "What an amazing blend of herbs and spices!" Tendigrads exclaimed.

"Yeah, there's eleven of them," Tommy said with a chuckle. Tendigrads stared in wonder at the light flooding from the ceiling, and the walls covered in ultra-bright red tile. Several people had come in during the evening rush, so more than a few customers were in the dining area.

Tendigrads saw a woman and three kids sitting at a table. She was quickly dispensing huge chicken legs, biscuits, and some pieces of paper to the extremely eager children. She had a beautiful green dress, and her hair was piled high upon her head, almost like a headdress. The two girls wore matching pink dresses, and the little boy had on a shirt similar in style to Talula's, but it had no writing. The boy paused from licking the honey off his biscuit to look up at Tendigrads. His sweet blue eyes opened wide, and he broke into a delighted squeal. Tendigrads smiled back; he always seemed to have a way with children.

Two men in their 30s were concentrating on their meal, not talking or looking at each other. A Native American couple in their 60s sat at a small table next to the counter. They also ate in silence, oblivious to the four newcomers.

The young man working the counter wasn't happy to be working at the KFC. He was sitting to the side of the cash register, reading a tattered copy of MAD magazine, and didn't even flinch when the door opened. Looking to be all of 17 years old, he read the last bit of his current page and reluctantly pitched the magazine aside. He fixed his elbows on the counter, chin in his hands, and muttered, "Can I help you?"

Talula started to speak, but Tommy interrupted. "We'll have two buckets of your finest chicken, Bobby, and a dozen biscuits, two orders of mashed potatoes and gravy, eight corn on the cob and four chocolate parfait buckets."

"Okay, Tommy. Don't break the bank here!" Talula exclaimed.

"Yeah, well, we got one bucket of dark meat, but it will be 15 minutes on more chicken," Bobby confided as he looked longingly at his magazine.

"Well, that will get us started. You can bring out the rest when it gets done," Talula said. She dug into her pocket for her coin purse, dumping a pile of change and bills on the counter.

Y'all want drinks? Bobby asked.

"Yeah, I'll pay for the drinks, Ta," Anson offered. He threw a dollar on the counter.

"That'll be fourteen dollars and fifty cents." They counted out dollar bills and quarters from Talula's pile, took their drinks and sat at a table next to the window.

Tendigrads had never used a straw before, so Talula tore one open, stuck it through the Coca-Cola lid, and handed it to him. The wizard saw his three companions sucking the cold drink through the straws, so he did the same. At first, he took a small sip. The cold liquid tickled going down, and although it was cold, it also had a pleasant burn and, finally, an explosion of sweetness. "Osda!" he exclaimed in his native tongue. And they all had a good laugh.

"That Coca Cola is pretty good stuff, isn't it, Master Tendigrads," Anson said as he reached for a chicken leg. Tendigrads took another big drink of his soda and nodded his agreement.

He had so many questions about all the different machines, airplanes, television, telephones and parking meters. The three young adults had questions for him as well. About magic, for the most part. But also about the differences between their two worlds.

They were on the edge of their seats as he described what he referred to as "The Fall" of the white civilization and the rise of "The First People."

They were full when the next bucket of chicken came out. So they sacked up all of the golden brown goodness and headed off to Talula's house. "Tomorrow we need to go back to the site and do one more very thorough search to see if we can find the octopod or any pieces of it. Maybe we can rebuild the pedestal somehow," Talula said from the back seat.

"We really dug through that pretty hard today, Ta, and we didn't find a thing," Tommy said.

"We need to be absolutely sure. If there is any part of that key or pedestal, we really need to find it so Tendi can look it over."

"Tendi! So when did he become Tendi?" Anson exclaimed. "I mean killer nickname, but it's the first I heard of it."

"Have you even okayed that nickname with him?" Tommy chided. They all looked at the old wizard who had his head out the window, looking up at the street lights with childlike wonder.

"Well, it's a lot shorter than Master Tendigrads. Tendi has a certain ring to it. What do you say?" Talula asked as she put her hand on his shoulder.

"I've been called that before," he answered, pausing to look around at his three companions. His eyes watered up. "You are most welcome to use that name." He patted Talula's hand.

Chapter Ten

They pulled into Talula's driveway. Her brand new 1975 Ford Maverick sat in the driveway where the tow truck driver had left it, taking up both spaces of the driveway.

"Do you have your key, Ta?" Anson asked.

"It's supposed to be on the porch under a brick," she said as she hopped out. She ran to the porch and returned holding up her key. "I'm all set! I'll come by your place tomorrow at 6:30 am so we can get an early start."

"Oh my god! 6:30? Have you lost your mind, Ta?" Tommy shouted.

"We all have to work at 4 pm tomorrow, so we have to get an early start, or we won't get anything done. Set your alarm, and I'll see you boys then," she said glaring at Tommy.

"We'll be ready," Anson assured her. He pulled out of the drive, and they rode back to the apartment in relative silence. Tendi was still looking out the window, studying all of this new and fantastic landscape, when he finally broke the silence.

"I fear you may be correct, Tommy," he said. "I looked for any hints of a portal, and I couldn't find anything through my methods. I had no idea I was looking for some sort of stone mechanism, but I suspect there will be little, if anything, left there that can help."

"Why are we going back then? I think we should have told her it was a waste of time." Tommy turned to look at the wizard.

"It is best to make sure. Miss Talula is a very bright young apprentice. She shows strong leadership and logic. I suggest we let her follow her instincts and support her decision."

"So you are saying she's bossy, and we should go ahead and let her have her way. Then when she realizes she is wrong, us guys can start working on getting this problem fixed!" He laughed as he slugged Anson in the arm.

"Dude, lay off," Anson said sullenly.

"Tommy, I was not trying to be humorous. I believe your friend has a great mind and definite magical talent. I can feel it in her aura. Much as I feel it in yours," Tendigrads said.

"Her 'aura'... Well, I don't know much about that... Oh, and you think I have magic powers, too! That's funny! Hey Rocky! Watch me pull a rabbit out of my hat!" Tommy said, in a poorly executed Bullwinkle the Moose's voice.

"Hmm, you have some ability; I feel it. But you also have some headstrong ideas that you might need to adjust," the wizard said. "One of my most important mentors was a young woman who had so much courage and wisdom that she made some men feel threatened. They missed the valuable gifts she could offer. I am grateful I chose not to be so blind."

Tommy turned back to look out the front window as the Plymouth pulled into their little driveway. He had never felt so eloquently chastised; Anson couldn't hide his grin. He was already in the Talula camp and was fast becoming a big fan of Tendi.

Chapter Eleven

A large male coyote was howling near the sand dunes north of Beaver. Somewhere very far off to the south, his mate answered. This old trickster had been in the world a few seasons. His hunting range had been plentiful for those seasons and, as far as a coyote's life was concerned, he had lived like a king. As he started to lope towards the sound of his mate, he caught the scent of something just ahead. Something he could eat. He sped up his gait until he came to the side of the road, and there he slowed down. One of the reasons he survived so many seasons was because he was smart, and although he had no concept of names like "road" he knew it was dangerous.

But there was often food on it or beside it. He listened. There were no roaring sounds to warn him of the huge beast that ran up and down the road. He sniffed the air; nothing but the slight smell of food. Confident in his safety, he walked over to the little rotten-smelling bones. As he lowered his snout to snap up the little treat, he made a muted screech as the reanimated hand that housed the kigatilik's life force clamped around the throat of the coyote. And just in time, as the kigatilik was fading and would have soon ceased to exist. But for now this demon from Tendigrads' world would be able to survive in the coyote until a more appropriate host could be found. The kigatilik craved the wizard who had burnt him so badly.

Chapter Twelve

The kigatilik was known in the mythology of the Inuit people as a clawed demon that hunted shaman for their magical abilities. But the kigatilik that appeared on the prairies of The First People's Land had extraordinary powers. Tendigrads' experience with these creatures was only through his discussion with elders, who had heard of these northern legends from a wandering pilgrim from the north-eastern lands. His information had led him to believe that the demon had evolved into something much more dangerous: A nightmare that was unusually powerful that could take the form of another being it had killed. Tendigrads had been summoned to Big Mounds to offer his perspective on the creature, as he was well versed in the demons and monsters of the native world. And so as Tendigrads headed out from Tahlequah to Big Mounds, he was aware of reports of a strange wolf-like creature that had been seen near his destination. He suspected it was the kigatilik.

Chapter Thirteen

At the apartment, the boys were introducing Tendigrads to their favorite evening tradition. They turned on the television right at ten-thirty and heard the opening orchestral arrangement of "Suicide is Painless." Tendigrads and the boys were on the couch watching the helicopters fly into MASH 4077. The wizard tried to keep in mind that this was just a new technology, but it sure seemed like magic to him. It was amazing to see the fuzzy but rather real looking figures in the wooden box that sat next to the front door.

"So Hawkeye and Trapper are the main characters in the show," Anson explained. "Now that little guy is..." But the old wand maker was already starting to fade. He'd had little sleep these past few days, and soon he was slumped over on the couch next to Tommy.

"Guess he's not big on MASH," Tommy said.

"Yeah, I guess he had quite a day," Anson added. The boys watched the rest of their show, turned the lights off, and crawled up to the loft for bed. Anson set the old wind up alarm clock for six o'clock in the morning. "God, that's early," he muttered.

"Yeah, but at least it's only supposed to be 98 degrees tomorrow," Tommy joked.

"Great, I'll wear my jacket!"

Talula's alarm went off at five o'clock. She gave a brief groan of bother and then got quickly out of bed. She threw an album on the turntable and started making sandwiches. "Time keeps on ticking, ticking, ticking, into the future," Steve Miller sang as she checked her family's well-stocked pantry. She grabbed some Fritos, Chips Ahoy cookies, two six-packs of sodas, Coke and Dr. Pepper, and ice. Then she loaded up the two Coleman coolers with water jugs, sodas, and sandwiches and put them in the trunk of her Maverick.

She wore elephant bell-bottom jeans and a white t-shirt with "The Rolling Stones" lips logo on the front, and a beat-up straw cowboy hat folded way up on the sides. She had already loaded all kinds of shovels, picks and other various tools in the trunk the night before so she could get an early start. She checked off all the items on her mental checklist and jumped in the Ford just after six o'clock. She hoped the boys were up, but she doubted it. She pulled out of her driveway and headed east on Fourth Street. The sun was starting to poke up on the horizon, and it blinded her, occasionally shining in her mirrors, so she grabbed her sunglasses from the glove box.

The only other vehicle on the road was the dairy truck pulling into Downing's Market. She turned into Helen Easton's driveway and eased back to the boys' apartment. She walked to the door expecting to have to rouse them all out of bed, but before she could knock on the door, Tommy swung it open.

"Good morning Ta. Do you need a cup of coffee?" Tommy asked cheerfully. He was fully dressed and ready to go.

"Morning Ta," Anson shouted from the loft.

"Good Morning," she shouted back as Anson slid down the ladder firemen style.

He grabbed his coffee and said, "Are we ready?"

"Yeah!" she said, surprised. "But where is Tendi?"

"He's out back. He said to come to get him when we're ready," Tommy said as he handed her a cup of black coffee with a splash of cream.

"Perfect, Tommy! Thanks!"

"I'll go get him, then we can hit the road," Anson said as he snagged his baseball cap off the table.

Tommy and Talula headed out to the driveway. "If you want to ride with me, I got it all loaded with tools and food. And it's got air conditioning," she said to sweeten the deal.

"Sounds good to me! It'll sure be good on the drive back," Tommy said.

"Osda Sanalei, Miss Talula," the wizard said as he walked up carrying a variety of sticks.

"Good morning to you, Tendi!" she exclaimed. She wasn't sure if she remembered the Cherokee phrase for good morning or if she just deduced that was his greeting. "What are all the sticks for?"

"They may not be of any use," he conceded. "But then again, I feel something special in these few I gathered."

"Let's take my car. Is that cool, ATV?"

"Yeah, that's great. I'm low on gas."

"Alright, well, let's roll."

They all piled into the Maverick with Tendi riding shotgun and the two boys in the back.

It was crowded in the car, but they only had about a thirty-minute drive out to the sand dunes. The morning was not yet too hot, and because they were so prepared, they found them-selves ahead of schedule. Talula put on an 8-track of "Car Wash" and started jamming out to the tunes as they zoomed up to Highway 270.

The boys were making their disco dance moves with their hands, and Talula smirked at them in the rear view mirror. Tendi-grads studied his sticks, took a small knife out of his pack, and began carving on them. Talula wasn't very pleased about all the wood chips on the floorboard, but she resisted saying anything. It looked a little like the old man was one with nature at the moment. She didn't want to break his Euell Gibbons' moment.

They pulled into the parking area, unloaded all their gear and brought it all up to the portal site. They sat for a moment, rested and talked.

"Okay, I think we need to at least sort through all this freshly broken rock and look for pieces of the octopod. Maybe we can find some pieces of the pedestal, too. We just need to be a little more systematic about it," Talula said. She reached into a small canvas bag and jerked out several small tent stakes and a ball of twine. "We can divide the area into smaller quadrants, so we are careful not to miss anything."

"Sounds good to me," Anson said.

"Good plan," Tommy agreed.

Talula smiled. She expected some resistance from Tommy, but he seemed very agreeable today, which made her feel relieved, as well as puzzled. "Okay, someone want to grab the hammer?" Anson had it in his hands before she could even finish.

They staked out the quadrants into ten sections and began painstakingly sifting through dirt, rock and sand. Tendigrads had his back to the group, and after about fifteen minutes, he held up a two-inch piece of reddish flint.

"I assume this was a piece of the octopod?" he asked. They all jumped up and ran over to the wizard to see what he had found.

"That's a piece of it! Groovy, Tendi!" Talula exclaimed.

"I don't see any sort of grooves or lines in this piece," he said.

The other three busted out in laughter. "'Groovy' is just a saying, Tendi. It means 'really good'," Anson said.

"Oh, well, it is always good to learn new languages." Then he was back at it.

It wasn't three minutes later that he had found another piece. "This appears to be part of the main body of the creature," he noted.

And they all jumped up again to see. He handed Tommy the piece and went back to work.

It was then that Talula saw the wizard's method for finding these pieces. He was using the wand that Talula had seen when he healed her. He was literally scanning the ground very slowly in straight lines back and forth over his search area. Within 30 seconds she saw a piece rise out of the sand and into his hands.

"Holy Mother of God," she whispered. Tommy and Anson were a little less amazed but still smiled in wonder.

"He's pretty amazing," Anson said.

Chapter Fourteen

Lawrence Carr was "walking in tall cotton." Not literally. He never picked cotton nor had his father before him, but the expression was so common in this part of the country that he had adapted it as one of his own.

If you asked Lawrence how he was doing, there was about a 73 percent chance he'd respond with, "Walking in tall cotton!" Lawrence owned Maxine's Fine Dining, which was only one of many of his business ventures. Maxine's was also the only one he could talk about with the good people of Beaver, Oklahoma.

He moved there in 1963 from New York and bought the little diner and eventually some property north of town. Lawrence was very good at gambling. In fact, he was one of those rare men who could win and know when to stop. However, his last bet in New York had not made him any friends. Lawrence didn't do anything illegal. He just made a bet with excellent odds that netted him $24,000, all thanks to a young man named Roger Maris. After Maris broke Babe Ruth's single-season home run record, young Lawrence became a very wealthy man, but the mob wasn't very happy about losing that much money. So after Lawrence picked up his winnings, he also received a tip that he'd better "get out of town." Lawrence was a smart young man and did just that. He was fond of the film "Oklahoma!" so he just jumped on a bus and headed that way.

Now Lawrence was a good cook. His mom was Italian, and he grew up around her in the kitchen. Fortunately, he was friendly and had tasty food, so folks in Beaver who would usually find a "Yankee" in their midst to be pretty undesirable took to Lawrence and his diner right off the bat. Lawrence eventually started his own under-the-table betting service with folks around town, and the sheriff didn't even flinch. Of course, he always ate for free.

Lawrence was walking to his white Lincoln to drive into town when he saw a coyote just standing there beside his car. Lawrence froze. He waited, expecting the animal to move on, but it just sat there staring at him. He tried to shoo the animal off, but it didn't budge. It was disconcerting how the creature just stared at him. Finally, Lawrence had enough and turned to go back to his house to get his gun. It occurred to him that the beast could be rabid, and he was taking no chances. As Lawrence opened the door to his house, he felt the bite of the coyote on his ankle. He screamed and kicked at the beast, and the coyote ran away as fast as it had appeared.

Lawrence stumbled into the house and grabbed his rifle, but by the time he stepped back outside, the coyote was gone. He limped out to the perimeter of the yard, but there was no sign of the beast. As he struggled back to the house, he became even more aware of the pain in his ankle. He laid the rifle on the porch, sat in his stamped metal chair, lifted the right leg of his pants and looked at his ankle. The wound was probably nothing more than a superficial puncture wound. It was barely bleeding at all now. However, the stinging was quite severe. "Oh, hell, I bet that damn thing had rabies," he muttered.

He put the rifle back in the house and limped out to the Lincoln. He was starting to sweat and felt a little dizzy as he pulled the car out of his circle drive and headed out onto the long gravel road that connects to Highway 23. Lawrence almost made it to the highway before he passed out, and the Lincoln rolled into a field and crashed into a grove of trees.

Chapter Fifteen

If there was one thing that Talula Polk hated, it was being the last one to know something. And seeing the knowing grins on Tommy and Anson's faces told her that she was out of the loop in their little secret.

"Alright, what gives?" she spat out with her arms crossed over her chest.

Tommy and Anson smiled again at each other.

"Well, Tendi believes he can teach you and me to use magic," Tommy said.

Tendigrads was still working his wand back and forth over his area, seemingly oblivious to the conversation going on right next to him. Talula was speechless. Her first instinct was to call bullshit, but it was kind of hard to do that with an old man sitting in the dirt next to her levitating rocks out of the ground.

"So, he is going to teach us all how to do magic?" Talula asked.

"There's another one," Tommy muttered as if to prove her point.

"Well, not me," Anson said somewhat sadly.

"Only those with the blood of The First People," Tendigrads explained. "But I have made the promise to show Anson some physical techniques with the long staff. And I don't know how much I can show you, but it is almost certain that you have the ability. We will see. I think I have found everything in my area, and I would suggest we stop for Alisdayvdi." They looked at him, waiting for his explanation. "Oh, what I mean to say is food!"

They sat on the small rock ledge where the pedestal had previously been and devoured the sandwiches Talula had made. Tendi was ecstatic to find Talula brought Coca-Cola in individual metal containers. He was just amazed with the drink, and he made a mental vow to learn to recreate it once he got back to his world.

When they had finished their early lunch, Tendigrads reached into his pack and pulled out two of the sticks that he had been carving in the car early this morning. One rod was a golden yellow wood with rough bark spots and yellow heartwood spirals exposed by exquisite carvings. A roughly polished malachite stone had been embedded into the thick end of the wood, and the finer end was rounded to a small, ribbed point.

The other one was created from a wood that alternated hues from dark brown to a golden auburn. This rod was completely free of bark and had an impressive pattern of hawks and stars carved in the thinner section. There were three tiny white stones set in the thick part of the stick. He handed this one to Talula.

"This wand is made of Redbud and is set with white buffalo gemstones. This wand should help with all manner of healing," Tendi offered. She took the wand and immediately felt a small spark of energy.

"Wow," she exclaimed as she looked up at Tendigrads with wide eyes.

He handed the other wand to Tommy. "This wand is made from Bois d'arc and is imbued with a malachite stone. This wand has an intriguing combination of characteristics," he said. "Malachite is a stone that makes it easier to feel compassion. When paired with Bois d'arc, it becomes a wand that offers protection against spiritual forces and helps in healing."

When Tommy took the wand, he felt nothing special at first, but then he felt a warmth from the wand that slowly increased, spreading up to his arm and chest.

"Well, that feels strange...and good!" Tommy said with wonder.

"Know this," Tendigrads began. "You must not use these simple spells that I show you for anything other than helping others. And from all you have told me about your world, I would strongly advise that you keep knowledge of these skills hidden. The results of the first set of spells I show you will not necessarily be very visual. Spells like Belief, Bless, Courage, Friends, Help, Protect and Safety offer a small amount of help that may not be seen for hours or days. But three of these spells, Laugh, Sleep and Cure, are generally fast-acting, while not instantaneous. Let's begin with the Laugh spell."

He grabbed his wand from its old hide case and began to trace the spell in the air. To Talula's surprise, the pattern and characters hung in the air in glowing green wisps of smoke or something smoke-like.

"Now, to enact the spell, you have to trace the pattern with your wand and speak the native word. Each syllable is attached to a movement of the pattern."

Tendigrads looked at Talula and waved his wand "U - ye - tsa – s - gv," he spoke each syllable happily. Talula looked at him for a moment and then burst out laughing. It was so natural, but she had no idea why she was laughing.

"He did that to us all morning," Anson said.

"Yeah, we would get as stone-faced as we could, and Tendi would cast that spell, and we would be laughing our tails off," Tommy added.

Talula finally gathered herself and exclaimed, "Amazing!"

"Now you will attempt to cast the spell on Tommy. Tendigrads instructed. "Go ahead, Talula."

She looked at the words still hanging in the air, traced the words and spoke the syllables. They waited, but nothing happened.

"Try again, but this time think of laughter. Any spell you might cast will need a certain amount of your own expression to deliver the effect."

She tried again, and this time could feel that her fluidity was much better. Tommy gave a small chuckle.

"Excellent," Tendigrads encouraged.

"Tommy, did you laugh on purpose?" Talula asked.

"Nope. I was trying like hell not to laugh."

"Unbelievable! I mean, this is just totally unbelievable!" she muttered.

"Tommy, try to cast the spell on Talula." Tommy took his wand and studied the words and the pattern. He focused and cast the spell with a happy, fluid motion.

"U - ye - tsa – s - gv!" At first, nothing happened, but then the stone-faced Talula quickly broke down and laughed as vigorously as she had before.

"Wonderful, Tommy! As I said before, I felt this ability in you. It is most likely also in those of your land who have the blood of The First People. Now, you must memorize the words and the pattern. You and Talula practice while Anson and I work on recovering more fragments."

Tendigrads went back to his bundle of sticks and pulled out a tall staff. It was about 5ft tall with a spiral twist carved in the top with a small exposure where a rough quartz crystal jutted out from the top. He handed it to Anson. "This staff is made from black locust. Do you know this wood, Anson?

"Yeah, it's got those nasty thorns all over it. I mean, the trees have thorns."

"Yes, it is one of the trees of both our worlds. But more importantly, it is a very strong wood. It also offers some protection from shadow magic. As we discussed, I don't sense any magical abilities in you, Anson, but that doesn't mean you cannot use items of magical ability."

Tendigrads took his knife out and grabbed the staff. "Do you see the knot in the wood just below the spiral twist? If you pull that knot away with a knife, you can release the crystal and place another imbued stone in its place." Tendi placed the knife in the spot and released the crystal. He then produced a dingy gold stone and placed it in the cavity.

"Now, Anson, I want you to slowly move the top of the staff over the ground and let me know when you feel the staff tug." Anson did as instructed, slowly moving the staff over the ground. After a few passes, he stopped.

"I think I felt it tug!" he said. "It's hard to tell, but I think I did."

"Make an X on the spot and continue," Tendigrads said as he leaned down to the area Anson was marking. The wizard focused his wand on the spot, and a shard of flint rose from the dirt.

"Thank you, Anson. We will make fast work of this now." He placed the fragment in an old Cain's coffee can Talula had retrieved from the car earlier.

After about 15 minutes of listening to Talula and Tommy laughing, Tendi showed them a second spell. He began to trace the spell in the air as before and motioned the two young folk to stand beside him.

"The next spell is called Cure, and it is a very simple four-move pattern. The Cherokee is enunciated as before, with each syllable merged to a movement of the wand. This spell can be taxing as a small amount of your own energy is expelled when casting this spell. So I want you to practice without targeting each other. Practice the movements while speaking the syllables under your breath."

He returned to the last patch of dirt to find Anson had five X's on the ground. He worked his wand over the X's and pulled the flint pieces out of the land. Tendi looked at Anson, who appeared more than exhausted and gave him a nod and a grin.

"Get some water, Anson," Tendi said. As the young man walked off, Tendi muttered an incantation of Cool Air over the young man. Tendigrads walked over to the broken rock pedestal and studied the corner of flagstone jutting out of the ground.

He looked the area up and down and noticed a scorpion crawling under the stone. Tendigrads looked at the small crack where the scorpion had gone and saw a rather large space beneath the flagstone.

He paused for a moment, then began to chant in his native tongue. He raised his arms and began to chant louder. The three young apprentices stopped and walked over to the old wand maker.

The massive stone was rising from the ground as Tendigrads held his hands above his head, moving his wand in the air. The stone started to lean over so that the bottom of the rock was exposed. The wizard slowly lowered his hands, and the massive rock came to rest. On the verge of collapse, the old wizard stumbled over to the rock and brushed away the dirt on the freshly exposed stone top. The others crowded around to see the shallow imprint of an octopod in the rock.

Chapter Sixteen

A 1960's Chevy Apache pickup truck was rolling down the gravel road kicking up an enormous amount of dust. You could hear a song blasting out of the old, half-green, half-primer truck.

"I never read it in a book; I never saw it on a show.
But I heard it in the alley on a weird radio."

Mack and Harlan Whitaker were singing at the top of their lungs, their chins jutting in perfect time as they blazed down the gravel road towards Highway 23. The brothers had been listening to this particular 8-track tape since Harlan bought it in '73, so they knew exactly when the odd fade would happen where the tape had to change tracks. "Ka Thug!" went the tape player, and the two young men froze. As the music quickly faded in, they were right on the downbeat, singing in perfect unison.

"If you want a drink of water,
You got to get it from a well,
If you want to get to heaven,
You got to raise a little hell."

It was no accident that they sounded so good. Mack and Harlan were fine musicians. The boys had played all over Texas and Oklahoma in country bands since they were old enough to drive. Mack was the steel player everyone wanted. He had even subbed out for the great Leon McAuliffe with Bob Wills and The Texas Playboys. Harlan was one year younger at 25, but he was as good a guitar player as anyone in either the Texas or Oklahoma Panhandle. Their great love of music had always been their single focus in life. The boys had just pulled out of Mack's house about two songs before, so it took a moment for them to take in the sight framed by the windshield.

At first, it didn't appear to be that big of a deal, just Mack's neighbor, Lawrence, pulling his big old Lincoln out on the road. He was going pretty slowly, which was not unusual, but then a coyote jumped out on the road sprinting after the Lincoln like it had missed its bus! The Lincoln was slowing and weaving, and the coyote seemed to be oblivious of the truck tailing behind him. Then the coyote did the strangest thing. It tried to jump up through the driver's side closed window. Almost like it was trying to attack the driver.

"Holy shit! Are you seeing that, Mack?" Harlan shouted.

"What the... that coyote is crazy, must be rabid! Grab that pistol out of the glove box, Harlan!" Matt hollered.

The Lincoln kept wallowing erratically down the gravel road like a wounded cow with the coyote harassing behind. The vehicle then started to pull to the right and eventually went into the ditch and ran over the fence. Mack slowed up and followed the car right into the bone-dry field.

The Lincoln rolled a bit further and slowly ran into a small grove of willow saplings growing near the dry creek bed. As the boys pulled up from behind, they saw the coyote howling and snapping at the window of the car. Harlan stepped out of the truck. Just as the coyote turned to look at them, he fired a shot from the little 22 pistol and hit the coyote.

They heard the animal yipping, but it ran farther into the field, as if its tail were on fire. The men ran over to the car that was nose down in the creek bed with its rear axle off the ground and its back tires still turning. Mack opened the door and saw Lawrence slumped unconscious in the front seat. He turned off the key and tried to wake Lawrence.

"Come on, buddy! Hey Lawrence, come on, man."

"He's out of it, Bro. We better get him to the hospital.

Together, the brothers pulled Lawrence out of the car and dragged him to the pickup. They sat him up between them, then Mack pulled the truck around and headed for town.

"He is burning up!" said Harlan.

"Yeah, I know," muttered Mack. "I hope it ain't catching."

Chapter Seventeen

"Oh my god, how did you know it was there?" Talula whispered as she traced her fingers in the dirty grooves of the great stone. Tendigrads was leaning up against it, exhausted from the powerful spell he had cast.

"Deduction for the most part, and then I was able to feel the faint magic in the stone. There were no large rock pieces in this area, so I thought maybe the pedestal fell over or sunk into the ground. When I saw the scorpion crawling under the rock, I suspected that the pedestal had indeed sunk into the ground after the explosion.

"So it looks like if we can get that octopod put back together, you can go home!" Anson announced as he looked for confirmation from his friends.

"It is possible, but repairing the key will be a challenge," Tendigrads said. Even if it is possible, I fear it is unlikely that the key will have retained its magic."

They all fell silent, reflecting on the possibility that the old wizard might not make it home. The three young friends could feel his sadness, but no one knew what to say.

"But, we must try, nonetheless!" he finally said as he rose to stand and inspected the indentation in the rock. "I think we are done here for today," he said as he retrieved his coffee can of small rock shards.

They loaded up the car with their gear and headed back to Beaver at around two o'clock. The heat was really coming on, and they were all happy to have the air conditioning blowing through Talula's Maverick.

"We should have time to get a shower before work and maybe even a nap!" Tommy calculated.

"Yes, I really can't believe we accomplished so much out there," Anson added.

"Yeah, it was almost like... Magic!" Talula quipped. And they all laughed.

"A delightfully wry assessment, Miss Polk," Tendigrads offered.

"Why, thank you, Tendi," she said with a comical Southern drawl as she touched the brim of her cowboy hat.

Talula pulled the Ford past Helen's house and into the back to drop off the guys. Before she could pull out, Helen was waving her down.

"Maxine's is closed tonight, boys. Mr. Carr is in the hospital, and I don't know when it will reopen. Her eyes were red from crying, and she was visibly shaken. It was unsettling to see the normally strong Helen Easton upset.

Tommy hopped out and stood beside Helen, and the woman leaned against him as she started to weep.

"Let's get out of the heat," Anson suggested.

"Yes, of course," Helen agreed as her sobs subsided. "Please come in."

It was at that moment that she finally noticed the old man in the John Deere hat. "Hello, and who is this?" she asked with a hint of suspicion.

"Ebrnt Tendigrads, Miss, but you can call me Tendi; I am honored to make your acquaintance," he answered as he put his hand on the brim of his hat, a move he had learned earlier from Talula.

Helen studied the old man for a moment. He was a ruggedly handsome senior fellow, and she was intrigued by his politeness.

"Tendi is my mom's uncle," Tommy explained, hoping he had their story straight.

"Rosa's uncle! Well! How nice to meet you! I don't remember you being at the funeral. Did I miss you somehow?"

"Unfortunately, I was unable to be there, one of the deepest regrets in my life."

"Let's all go inside. I have a pitcher of lemonade in the fridge."

They went inside and sat down while Helen shuffled over to the cupboard to get some glasses.

"Let me help with this, Mrs. Easton," Talula suggested. Helen looked at Talula with tired eyes.

"Surely. The glasses are over there." Helen pointed. She walked over to her old, round oak table, joined the others, and grabbed her cigarettes, holding the pack out to Tendigrads, who politely declined. She lit one and took a quick drag before slumping back in her chair.

"Well, it doesn't look real good for Lawrence," she confided. "He has been bitten by a coyote, but he shows all the signs of being poisoned. They can't figure out what's wrong with him. The Whittaker brothers were driving behind him when he swerved off into a field and crashed. And here is the crazy part; a coyote was chasing the car. One of the boys shot the coyote, but it ran off somehow. He must have just winged it. Anyways, they found a bite mark on Lawrence's ankle, but the mark wasn't that bad. It looks like the coyote was poisoned somehow. In fact, the doctor said it looks more like a giant rattlesnake bite. That's exactly what the doctor told me. He is really sick, and they don't know what to do." Her eyes started to water up again.

Talula gave everybody a glass of lemonade and grabbed a yellow metal stool from the corner of the tight little kitchen. Tommy and Anson were still trying to put all this together. They liked Mr. Carr. He was always pretty good to them, and from what Helen was saying, things sounded shaky for the owner of Maxine's Fine Dining.

"We need to go see Mr. Carr," Tommy said decisively. "Don't you think, Talula?"

"Umm, yes, we should go see him," Talula slowly agreed.

"I don't think you can see him; he is quarantined until they have more information. Whatever he has might be contagious," Helen said.

"Let's go, guys," Tommy announced decisively, as he stood up. The others followed his lead and started heading out the back door.

"Wait, I would like to go, too," Helen said as she grabbed her purse off the arm of her kitchen chair.

"Sure, Mrs. Easton, but it's going to be a little tight in the Maverick with five," Talula offered.

"Well, Mr. Tendigrads and I can take my car," Helen replied as she looked at Tendi.

"Excellent suggestion!" Tendigrads agreed. Tommy noticed a rare smile from Mrs. Helen Easton as they walked out the back door.

Chapter Eighteen

Coyote was lying in an old irrigation pipe underneath a dirt driveway leading to an oil field. It could hear the rhythm of the strange machine that looked like a bird repeatedly dipping its bill into the ground. Coyote's wound was mortal, and it took all the kigatilik had to keep the life force in place. The creature recalled the early memories of the lands of ice. Ice and cold. It craved ice and cold. The kigatilik remembered when it hunted the Inuit in the ice and cold. And the time when the world of ice fell into the sea. The snow was gone, and the demon floated without a physical body until it was finally able to enter fish. Then it swam for an extended period until kigatilik allowed itself to be caught by Bear. When the fish entered its belly, Bear ceased to exist.

And so it took Bear and walked across the green forests with the vast trees. This new land was not cold and icy, but there were so many magical creatures. Mostly shadow magic, which was a new experience.

And so it feasted and grew stronger. And its hunger became strong. But creatures feared Bear even more than before, and the magical creatures could sense the dark presence as it grew stronger. And so the demon pushed south. Even though going south led to more heat, it learned that when Bear's body was not fed, it was difficult to move. And eventually, Bear could not move anymore. And the wolves came. When the wolves attacked, it was able to bite one and move to Wolf. And the kigatilik joined in with the other wolves in eating the corpse of Bear.

Wolf was a much better host. Wolf was fast and had great endurance. Wolf was a silent and deadly hunter. And so it hunted, but there was little magic in the land. The kigatilik could sense there was magic further south. The south meant more heat, but there was strong magic there that it craved. It ran further south and finally came to a land with more magic.

Once again, dark magic, but also a new sort of magic. Stronger than in the Inuit. The kigatilik couldn't wait to feast, but these creatures were not ones to fall to its fearful aura. They fought and hurt it. So it became more selective, hunting down the two-legged creatures when they were alone. The demon eventually took the form of one of these creatures, which made it much easier to trick them.

So when it sensed one of these creatures alone on the trail, it closed with frightening speed. The creature was old, but it held powerful magic. The kigatilik sprang on the two-legged creature as he walked slowly up the path in the bright sun.

But the creature was surprisingly fast. And the creature made a terrible light that burned the kigatilik's senses and blocked its fearful aura. It cast the blackness to counteract the burning light and chased the creature. Just one taste of flesh, one blooding of its fingernails, and it would own the magic. The kigatilik rushed towards the old creature; they both fell through a flash of green light. And when the green light went out, it felt itself burnt by the hottest thing imaginable. And then nothing.

But the demon eventually became aware again and knew that this was another world. A world of the most extreme heat it could imagine. But it had just enough power to pull its remains together enough to find a new host. Coyote should have been a suitable host, but the bite on the first two-legged creature did not take, and in its hurry to chase the creature down, it was struck again by fire in coyote's side. And so the kigatilik would

need to find another host before its dark life force was extin-
guished.

These were the thoughts that passed through its mind as the
rumbling of some great beast above its head caused dirt to shake
down over coyote's bloody, matted fur.

Chapter Nineteen

The drive to the hospital was mostly uneventful for Helen and Tendigrads. There was a bit of confusion when Tendi had to explain why he wouldn't drive Helen's 1972 Buick Skylark to the hospital. When she asked him if he would mind driving, Tendigrads was taken by surprise.

"I am unable to," he replied.

"What's the matter? Did you forget your glasses or something?" she smiled.

"Yes," he answered with confidence.

"Well then," she said with a shrug. "I'll drive."

As they pulled onto the street, she tried to strike up a conversation. "So where do you call home, Mr. Tendigrads?"

"Tahlequah."

"What do you do in Tahlequah?"

"I am at the university. I instruct people in Cherokee history."

"Oh! Are you Cherokee?"

"Yes, I am Cherokee, and I had ancestors in Ireland."

"Irish! I'm Irish as well," Helen said. "My maiden name is Murphy."

"Helen Murphy, a beautiful name," he said with a smile.

"So you speak Cherokee, Mr. Tendigrads?"

"Yes, I do."

"I would love to hear you speak in Cherokee if you wouldn't mind."

He paused and then spoke a phrase: "Hilayvi udehnvi dagi dunyatalohiyvhi ani yvwiya. Uhnee osda i dagi tsehlu Ani yvwiya udlohyilvi." It sounded magical to Helen.

"What does that mean in English?"

"Something like 'When you were born, you were crying, and everyone else was smiling. Live your life so that at the end, you're the one who is smiling, and everyone else is crying.'"

She glanced over at him in wonder.

"Well, that is just a beautiful sentiment," she said in her South Boston accent.

She patted his hand gently as she stopped the car in the hospital parking lot.

Talula and the boys pulled in right behind them. "Well, I wonder how those two are getting on," Talula remarked. "I have a feeling there is something brewing there."

Anson looked at her quizzically. "What do you mean?" he said.

"Oh, nothing," she replied as they climbed out of the car.

Tommy was already jogging over to Tendigrads and Helen.

"So, what is the plan?" he asked, looking at the wizard.

"I think we should go in and see what we can do for your friend," Tendigrads replied.

"They won't let you near him, Tommy." Helen repeated. "Someone is guarding the door of his room."

"We need to see him; we might even be able to help him," Tommy explained. At that moment, Talula and Anson walked up to join them.

"So any ideas, Tendi?" Anson asked.

"Yes, it won't be too difficult getting into the room if Anson can cause a brief distraction. I will conceal the four of us right before the door to your friend's room."

"Conceal?" Helen questioned, "How are..."

"Anson, you will need to walk by the door and quickly open it and hopefully get whoever is guarding the entrance to chase you down the hall a bit until we can go in.

"I can do that," Anson acknowledged.

"Now wait a minute..." Helen tried to interject.

"We all need to hold hands just before I cast the illusion. If you let go, if you try to touch anything or anyone touches you, then you will become unconcealed. Once we are in the room, we can attempt to help your friend."

"What kind of craziness are you kids involved in?" she demanded.

"Helen, I know it sounds nuts, but Master Tendigrads can absolutely do everything he says he can. We have witnessed his work all day today," Talula said.

"If I had heard any of this two days ago, I would be right with you, Helen, but it is absolutely true," Anson added.

Helen's thoughts raced. She was sure these kids had been duped. And apparently, so had she. "Still falling for the crazy ones," she muttered.

"If we don't get into the room, then you are positively correct in your assessment of my abilities, Helen," Tendigrads said. "So I propose a wager. If I cannot get us inside Mr. Carr's room, then I will happily leave you and these young people alone. However, if we are able to complete our objective, I propose that you take us all to the Colonel's Chicken Shoppe. I have a strong desire for his 11 herbs and spices and a Coca-Cola."

"You are a madman," she finally said in hushed astonishment.

"On the contrary, I am not upset with anyone," the wizard said. "But I have an idea that we need to take action now to save your friend."

"Fine," she finally conceded. "You have a bet." She stuck out her hand begrudgingly to Tendigrads, and they shook.

They headed into the small, one-floor hospital, and Tendigrads motioned to a young nurse sitting in an old fiberglass school chair, reading a book. Just across the hall was the nurse's station with two nurses who seemed to be busy with some sort of paperwork.

"Remember, hold hands, and do not touch anything. Don't let anything or anyone touch you." Tendi reminded them. "Proceed, Anson."

Anson walked quickly past the nurse at the doorway, turned around, and carefully put his hand on the doorknob. He gave it a turn and discovered that it was unlocked. He swung the door open, and the young nurse jumped up.

"You can't go in there," she said.

She reached to close the door, and Anson put his foot in the way. The woman tugged at the door and started yelling at Anson. "Hey! Move your foot!" Anson then snatched the book out of her hand and started waving it around.

"Catch me if you can!" he taunted. The furious young nurse was off and running after him, down the hallway towards the rest of the group.

Just before Anson had opened the door, the four companions held hands as Tendigrads made a pattern in the air with his wand and muttered, "A-dis-ga-lo-di." They were concealed.

Tendigrads led them down the hall. He steered them to the right wall as Anson and the young nurse came running past. Then the other two nurses followed them. None of the nurses noticed the four of them creeping by and holding hands. Helen wondered why the nurses didn't even glance at them. She could obviously see her group. They continued to the door, and Tendigrads paused.

"You first, please, Helen. You can let go of Talula's hand. She did as instructed and went into the room. Mr. Carr lay in the bed with a tube stuck down his throat, all kinds of machines around him, and an IV stuck in his arm. She looked back at the others, but they weren't there. She stepped out quickly to look for them and ran right into an invisible Talula.

"Ow! Helen! The rest of the group became visible immediately. Now Helen was completely speechless. Open-mouthed, she stared at Tendigrads.

The wizard moved to the bed as Talula closed the door and put her index fingers to her lips. "Shhh," she whispered and then added, "Chicken is on you tonight, Mrs. Easton." Helen was dumbfounded.

Tendigrads put his hand on Mr. Carr's head. He was burning with intense fever. After a moment, Tendi muttered "shadow poison," and everyone could feel his concern. "This is bad news."

He continued to examine Mr. Carr and found the wound coyote had left. After studying the wound, he turned to Talula and Tommy.

"I will need your assistance," he said, drawing the cure spell in the air for the two apprentices to see. This was just too much for poor Helen. She moved to a chair beside the bed, sat down and rubbed her eyes in disbelief. "Dear Lord Jesus," she quavered.

Tommy and Talula produced their wands and awaited instructions.

"I just need you to cast the cure spell on the bite wound." Tendigrads said. "Keep chanting it until I stop. It's superficial now but still needs to be treated. I will handle the shadow poisoning."

The three worked on Mr. Carr for about five minutes when the wizard finally stopped.

He reached up to feel Mr. Carr's forehead and smiled after a moment. "He will be fine; there is no fever now." Helen jumped up at this and touched the man's forehead. It was as normal as could be. Helen locked eyes with Tendigrads and finally went to him and hugged him, crying with joy.

"I don't know who you are, but God bless you, sir."

66 ~ GREGG STANDRIDGE

Chapter Twenty

Karl Schmidt drove his brand new Ford pickup over the cattle guard that led to his land. One hundred sixty acres that he used to try to farm before Skelly Oil changed his fortunes. Now there were 27 oil wells on his battered old farmland pumping up about $200,000 a year right into his bank account. With that much money, you would think that life would be easier. He could buy just about anything he wanted and purchase the best cars, guns, boots, and whiskey. Hell, he even had money to pay his way out of driving drunk. He had made many donations to the "Special Police Fund" over the years since his Henry had died.

Karl wasn't a friendly drunk, not that he was all that friendly before he started drinking. People felt sorry for him, but no one wanted anything to do with him. Everyone steered clear of Karl Schmidt.

He pulled the truck into his field and parked it with the truck bed pointing towards the pump jacks. Each one pumped up about 8 gallons of crude with each stroke. They reminded him of those stupid plastic drinking birds that The Horseshoe Club used to have sitting on their bar, bobbing into water glasses with their little top hats. He didn't care though, because his "oil birds" were making him rich.

He killed the ignition, grabbed his brown bag holding a brand-new bottle of Jim Beam and his Winchester .30-06 with three boxes of shells, and climbed into the truck bed.

One of the "upgrades" he had put in his truck was an all-weather recliner in the bed. He knew the town idiots laughed about it, but he couldn't care less. He set the whiskey and shells on the metal table that he had welded to the inside of the truck bed and sat down with his rifle across his knees to begin his evening ritual.

He reminisced about Henry. He thought about his wife, Jane. He thought about his time in the army and how he had been denied the chance to see "real action." His dismal service experience was at the POW camp in Alva. He had dreamed of going to Germany and fighting his evil cousins to show everybody in his home town that he wasn't a "Stinking Kraut." But after joining, he was stationed just over one hundred miles from Beaver. To make matters worse, he was guarding German POWs.

He took out his frustration on the prisoners whenever he could, and they hated him because of his name. Eventually, his anger took him too far, and he beat one of the prisoners so severely that he was disciplined and removed from duty. He made a deal and took a general discharge rather than face a court martial. He told everyone back home that he had received an honorable discharge.

Jane was his high school sweetheart and had loved him despite his temper. Karl softened when Henry was born; it changed him for the better. Everybody loved Henry, and no one more than his father. When he wasn't in school, Henry was right by his father's side, learning how to repair trucks, tractors, cars, or just about anything of a mechanical nature. One of Karl's redeeming qualities was his skill as a mechanic. Schmidt Mechanical was the most reputable repair shop in the Oklahoma Panhandle.

When the conflict in Vietnam broke out, Karl started talking about his time in World War II. He reminisced about the imaginary great times he had in the army. His only regret was not seeing combat. Jane would cringe at these rants and try anything to change the subject. Henry was listening, and as soon as he was able, he joined the army.

Karl couldn't have been prouder. His son would continue on the path that was taken from him, and after that, he would come back and work the shop with his dad. Henry left for Fort Polk, Louisiana, on October 07, 1966. That was the last time Jane and Karl saw their son. An accident in basic training took his life only six weeks after he left.

Jane was destroyed, as was Karl, and she was silent for almost a month. But one night, she couldn't keep it in any longer, and she unleashed her anguish on Karl. She blamed Karl for Henry's death and told him that she would never forgive him. And that is the kindest way to express what was said that night. Karl went to The Horseshoe to drown his sorrows, and he found plenty of sympathy at first. But eventually he became the guy that folks took bets on to see how fast he got thrown out of the bar.

So here he was, taking swigs of Jim Beam and shooting at imaginary German soldiers in his oil patch. He would do it until he was numb, then his oil birds and the whiskey would sing him to sleep.

Chapter Twenty One

Helen handed Bobby Guthrie a $20 bill, and he handed her change back with as little enthusiasm as possible. His "magazine du jour" was an Archie comic half-soaked in chicken grease. She rolled her eyes at the young man and put her change back in a leather coin purse with a Western motif engraved on its side. Anson and Tommy had already grabbed the food and taken it to a table. There were no other customers in the KFC, so they were free to talk about the day's events.

Of course, it was Helen asking the bulk of the questions. All the who, what, why, where and when's, and the big one, the how.

"So, you're telling me that you came here through some sort of time portal that our Talula here happened to open with a stone octopus?"

"I believe you understand it perfectly," Tendi said as he raised his head from the tall cup of Coca-Cola.

"And we have the pieces of the octopod. So we just need to try to put it back together. If we can do that, then we might get the portal back open, and Tendi can get back to his own world," Tommy explained.

"I think we have another problem that will need to be addressed before we worry about that, Tommy. Mr. Carr's poisoning was not of your world. It was shadow magic, I am sure. I believe the kigatilik has somehow passed through the portal with me. I will have to find it and destroy it before I can leave."

This news cast a dark mood over the group; as Tendigrads explained more about the creature, they grew more fearful.

"So if this creature takes control over its victims when they're bitten, how come it didn't take control of Mr. Carr?" Talula asked.

"Did you notice the purple stone in Mr. Carr's ring?" Tendi asked.

"Sure! I don't know where he got it, but it is an amethyst." Helen answered.

"Yes, and we need to find some pieces of this gem, especially for Talula and Tommy, as this creature feeds on magic and magic users." The old man sat there for a moment, and his eyes began to close.

"Are you alright, Tendi?" Anson asked.

'I have expended just about all of my energy today. If it is agreeable with everyone, I request that we return to the lodge."

The three young friends considered all of the astounding things this man had accomplished today. It was no wonder he was exhausted.

"Sure, Tendi. Let's head home," Anson said as he started gathering trash off the table.

"I will check in with you in a little while," Helen said, moving quickly to the door. She was gone so fast that the others had no time even to say goodbye.

"Wow, she's got a bee in her bonnet! I wonder what got into her?" Talula asked.

"I bet she is going back to see if Mr. Carr is awake," said Tommy.

"We'd better get him home." Anson pointed to the wizard slumped in the corner, gently snoring.

Chapter Twenty Two

Jane Schmidt was sitting on her couch watching *The Carol Burnett Show* on her brand new VHS player. It took her some time to figure out all the workings of the machine, but now she could tape all her favorite shows and watch them repeatedly. *Happy Days*, *All In The Family* and *The Waltons*, to name a few.

She would leave a note for Karl when she needed blank tapes, and he placed them on the kitchen table. Or she would just call any shop in Beaver, and they would put anything she needed on credit. But Jane didn't need that much, only the VHS tapes, some Frescas, and of course, her prescription. "Thank god for Valium," she often thought.

Jane's home was expansive, to say the least. With five bedrooms, four baths, two living areas, a massive den, and a guest house that she used for her jewelry and craft workshop. There was plenty of room to avoid Karl. She had just gotten up from the couch to get another Fresca and some cheese and crackers when she heard a knock at the door.

She could see Helen Easton at the door and cursed a bit. She looked at her hair in the mirror by the door, gave up quickly and cracked the door open.

"Helen! I wasn't expecting you!" She said through a forced smile.

"Of course not, I would have called, but you never answer your phone, so I just dropped by."

"Oh," Jane muttered, looking a little hurt.

"I really need to talk to you," Helen said. "It's important, or I wouldn't bother you."

Jane looked at her quizzically and opened the door for her friend.

"Come on in then." Jane's weekly ritual was pretty much the same every week, and the only time she ever went anywhere was to fill her prescription or pick up Helen for church on Sunday.

"Want a Fresca?" she asked as she headed for the kitchen.

"No, I just had a soda."

"Why aren't you working today?" She popped the top of her drink can.

"Mr. Carr had an accident and is in the hospital."

"What! What in God's name?" Jane exclaimed, reaching for her cigarettes.

"He's going to be okay," Helen assured her. "An animal bit him."

"Well, I am very happy to hear that. So what do you need, Helen?"

"Well, first of all, do you have any amethyst in your jewelry stuff?"

"Yes, I do."

"I need to make some amethyst necklaces, six to be exact."

"Sure, that's no problem. I can get them to you by this weekend," she said as she flicked ashes into a cast iron, Texas-shaped ashtray.

"I know this is a lot to ask, but I need them now."

"Helen! What the hell! I don't even know where all that stuff is."

"I have to have them now. If I tried to explain...well. I promise I will explain it all, just not right now. Look, I'll even help you. And pay you double what you usually charge."

"Pfff." Jane flicked her cigarette. "Let's go to the workshop. I'm scared to ask about the second thing you wanted."

"Is your nephew still in school down in Norman?"

"Robert? Yes, he is studying archaeology."

"That's what I thought. Do you have his number? I need to talk to him about an artifact that the boys found out by the sand dunes."

"Well, sure, Robert is just a sweetheart," Jane said. "I'm sure he'd be glad to help the boys. Alright, let's go make these necklaces so I can get back to my shows."

Chapter Twenty Three

Spider made her web in a tunnel in the end of a pipe running under the driveway where Coyote lay. And when Coyote hit the web and ruined all her hard work for the day, Spider decided this rude fur bearer would need to be taught a lesson. And so as Coyote was taking its last ragged breaths, Spider crawled down the ribbed metal walls of the pipe and dropped down on Coyote. She found a place just inside Coyote's ear and bit into the animal. As she did, she felt a strong, dark force enter into her small black body. And then her tiny spirit was no more.

The kigatilik assessed the new host with a mix of disgust and relief. In only a moment, Coyote would have faded; not much longer after that, the kigatilik would have faded as well. Spider was a horrible host, but fate had been with the kigatilik. For the spider's bite was the only chance it had to invade this host.

And so spider crawled out under its command. Such a slow, frail body. Likely many nights would pass before finding a suitable host. At least it was dark now; the heat was only insufferable. It crawled on towards a steady grinding sound and eventually saw a metallic wagon in which the two-legged creatures rode. It moved up to the wagon and instinctively released a web that caught high on the metal. Climbing up the web, the kigatilik finally reached the very top of the wagon and then looked down through its many eyes and saw one of the creatures. It took a moment to feel for any protective wards like the last one he had bitten carried. But there were no protective charms on this creature. And so it simply dropped down on the exposed neck and bit.

And so it was that Karl Schmidt was released from one painful existence only to become the vehicle of an even darker one.

Chapter Twenty Four

"I ain't got no hoooome,
I'm just a ramblin' round. Hard-working man,
I go from town to town,"

You could hear the voice coming from the battered old white building with a black number 6 on the side. It was once a naval barracks from World War II, but now it served as a storage catch-all for various forms of study subjects at The University of Oklahoma, OU.

"The police make it hard, wherever I may go,
and I ain't got no home in this world anymore."

The man continued to sing the Woody Guthrie tune as he picked on a mandolin to accompany himself. He was a lanky young fellow with dark curly hair that probably added about 4 inches to his 6-foot frame. Ruggedly good-looking, he was in blue jeans, moccasin boots, and a T-shirt that said, "Walnut Valley Festival."

Robert Bartlett packed up his mandolin in its case and checked the old building's doors before he left for his little apartment on Lindsay Ave. He really liked Norman and the park just across the street. He could often be found playing guitar at the duck pond and, of course, feeding the ducks.

But he also enjoyed his work-study job with the university. It allowed him time to practice and see a few interesting artifacts. In his last year at OU, Robert was hoping to land a job and stay on with the university.

He walked into his studio apartment at around seven o'clock that evening, and the phone was ringing. He set his case down on the bed and answered.

"Hello?"

"Hello, is this Robert?" It was a woman's voice.

"Yeah, this is Robert."

"Hi Robert, this is Helen Easton," the woman said. "I am a friend of your Aunt Jane's. I met you once a few years ago when you came up to visit."

" I remember you, Mrs. Easton. Is Aunt Jane okay?

"Oh yes, she's fine. She gave me your number because I have some young friends who could use your help. Would you mind talking to them?"

"Well, what do they need?" Robert asked.

"They have some questions about an Indian artifact they found," Helen said. "I'm going to hand the phone to Talula here."

"Hello, Robert." Talula got on the line.

"Hi, Talula. Tell me about this artifact."

Robert was expecting it to be an arrowhead or maybe some pottery shards. He had experienced this before with friends and family. Of course, there was always the piece of silver and turquoise jewelry handed down from a family member whose great-grandmother was an "Indian princess." He took it all in stride; that was just his nature. Bo, as his family called him, was the epitome of calm.

His work on the Calf Creek site had caught his professors' attention at OU, and they had nothing but praise for his work. Robert had seen the real thing when it came to native artifacts; he wasn't going to get excited about this one anytime soon.

"Well, I found this octopod-shaped stone in an old site just south of the sand dunes near Beaver," Talula began. "It's made of flint, and I am sure it's very old."

Despite himself, Robert was intrigued. What crazy thing had this girl found? She sounded sincere, but a stone octopod?

"So you found this yourself, in the ground at a site?" he said. "Why did you call it a site?"

"Well, I have dug up a lot of arrowheads and pottery shards in this area. It looked like it was an old, filled-in abandoned well," she said. "I discovered it about eight years ago, I guess."

This was not at all what Robert had expected; it actually sounded halfway interesting. But he had no idea why a stone octopus was doing in the panhandle of Oklahoma.

"That does sound interesting, but an octopod stone has little, if anything, to do with the native culture of the Great Plains," Robert pointed out. "I am not sure what you found, but I would love to see it."

"Well, we would like for you to see it!" Talula sounded excited. "But there is a little problem. The octopod stone was damaged in...in an accident. We are putting it back together as we speak."

Robert's enthusiasm started to fade at the mention of an accident.

"Was it intact when you pulled it out of the ground?" he asked.

"Yes! It was, and the carvings on this were truly amazing," she added.

"Well, how did you break it?"

"Well... um..."

At this point, Helen motioned for the phone. She took it and spoke quickly.

"Robert, do you know anything about the Shaman's Portal here in Beaver?"

"Yes, I know the legend of Coronado's men disappearing."

"Well, we have a visitor from the portal. Talula and her friends took that octopus thing out to the dunes and placed it in some markings on the rocks, and there were a bunch of green lights, and now we have this old Indian Shaman in our world."

Robert heard a voice in the background say, " 'First People,' Helen! Indian is not a respectful name!"

"First People," she corrected. Tendigrads smiled. "Now I know you don't believe any of this, but if you know anything about that portal or that octopus that could help us, then I am begging you. Could you help us? Come up to Beaver, and we can show you the proof.'"

Robert was absolutely silent. There was some mix of delusion and craziness going on up in Beaver that had driven poor Helen off the rails. Talula grabbed the phone back.

"Robert, I know it sounds crazy, but there is an indentation in a large stone at the sand dunes that perfectly fit the octopod stone. And when I placed the octopod in the indentation, Master Tendigrads came through the portal. I saw it with my own eyes. I am not crazy, and he is here, and he is an actual wizard. Or shaman. In other words, he can do magic. This is the most amazing archaeological discovery ever! Please believe me. We could use your help solving this mystery."

She was almost in tears. Her urgency was so compelling that Robert heard himself say. "Call me back tomorrow at seven o'clock, and I'll see what I can find out."

"Thank you! Thank you so much, Robert. We'll call tomorrow."

He hung up the phone and sat still on the bed, replaying the conversation over in his head. "That was way beyond weird," he muttered as he pulled off his boots. He made a PB&J in the kitchenette, grabbed a Sprite, and flipped on his TV. To his surprise, *The Twilight Zone* theme song was just beginning.

Chapter Twenty Five

Talula gave the phone back to Helen, and she hung it up in the cradle.

"What did he say?"

"He said to call him back tomorrow night."

"That's good!" Helen said.

"Yeah, but I don't think he believes us."

"Well, who would?" Anson exclaimed as he came closer to Talula, put his arm around her shoulder for just a moment, before he gave her a pat.

"You did great, Ta," he said. "And you too, Helen."

Talula patted his hand just before he took it away and smiled at him through her tears.

Tommy and Tendigrads were at Helen's kitchen table with the pieces of the octopod laid out in some order that only those two understood. They seemed to be making progress. About 10 of the 150 or so pieces had been cemented back together with jewelry cement that Helen had borrowed from Jane.

Helen reached in her bag and handed each of them an amethyst crystal with a simple leather string to tie around their necks. Tendigrads, who had taken a bit of a nap, was ecstatic at the gift. "Such a rare find in my land. What a kind and precious gift."

Helen wore one as well and insisted that Jane wear one also.

"What on earth for?" Jane had asked. To which Helen responded: "Jane, please do this for me. Don't ask questions; please just do it! It looks lovely on you."

"I think we should all stay together until we can resolve the issue of the kigatilik," Tendigrads looked at Helen with some concern. "I doubt it would openly attack me again, but it will be hunting us and looking for an opportunity to separate Talula or Tommy."

"Agreed, I will pull some blankets down for pallets. The boys can sleep on the living room floor. You can take the couch, Tendi, and Talula can take the spare room."

As everyone lay down to sleep, the old wizard spoke some words and waved his wand over each of them. "A simple ward of protection," he said as he lay down on the couch.

They were all asleep instantly, almost like magic.

Chapter Twenty Six

Karl Schmidt woke up from drunken sleep and took in the surroundings. He looked at the empty whiskey bottle and craved a swig. Such nonsense! The kigatilik would no longer allow that to affect its new host. It studied the long metal object lying across Its knees. Accessing Karl's brain, the demon understood that the object was a weapon. Very likely, the same sort of weapon that had ended Coyote. Once again, the kigatilik accessed the brain for knowledge on how to use the weapon. He lifted the rifle, opened the bolt action, popped a round in, and firmly put the stock to his shoulder. He squeezed the trigger and struck one of the pump jacks as a loud retort echoed through the air.

This was much better than Bear, Wolf, or Coyote. Karl would be an excellent host. The kigatilik sat and studied Karl. There was so much in this one's brain: The history of this land, the nature of mechanics, and the hatred for "idiots." Identifying idiots seemed to be an essential aspect of this host's existence. About that time, Karl, now the kigatilik, leaned over the side of the pickup bed to vomit before instinctively reaching for the bottle.

Lawrence Carr was walking across a wooden bridge in a strange forest land. A gentle snow was falling, and the temperature was cool. He was wearing cowboy boots, jeans, and a fur-lined Sherpa jacket. He also had a cowboy hat on, which was strange; he never wore a cowboy hat.

He walked across the bridge and looked down to see two men ice fishing in a river. As they waved, he recognized them as Babe Ruth and Roger Maris.

"Larry!" The Babe said. "I gotta say I sure wasn't pulling for ya when you bet on Roger this year, but if anybody was gonna break my record I'm glad it was him." Then he gave Roger a big bear hug.

"Alright, big fellow, let me down," Roger said with a grin. "Thanks for the confidence in me, Lawrence. I don't think I could have done it without you!"

After The Babe set Roger down, they started walking towards Lawrence and the bridge.

"Man, you dodged a bullet on that whole coyote thing. How did you survive that?" Roger asked. He pulled out a tin of breath mints. The Babe nudged his shoulder, and Roger dropped a couple into his outstretched hands.

"Yeah, I thought you were a goner, Larry. "How did you get out of the hot box, pal?" Babe asked.

Lawrence raised his right hand and showed them the amethyst ring.

"Oh!" The two legendary New York Yankees exclaimed in unison.

"That's some good magic there, Bub!" Roger emphasized with a couple of head nods.

Just then, Lawrence turned to find a limping coyote struggling across the bridge toward him, wounded and whimpering. The beast finally lay down, and Lawrence could see its life force crawl out of its body.

But then the life force slowly took the shape of a giant black spider. It was obviously a black widow, and it walked sideways back and forth with two of its front legs probing the air right in front of Lawrence's face. He screamed a silent scream as the multifaceted eyes locked in on him, but the behemoth ran away, squealing as Lawrence raised his ring.

The horrid creature began to writhe and spin; faster and faster, it whirred. The mass of black began to turn red and then slowed its spinning.

"You better hoof it, buddy!" Roger yelled.

But Lawrence couldn't move. He tried to run, but he had lost control of his legs. He watched in terror as the turning mass of horror finally came to a stop. And sitting there in his red truck was Karl Schmidt with a look of triumph on his face. For a moment, Lawrence thought Karl might have crushed the eight-legged monster with his truck, but then Karl stomped on the gas, and snow shot out from the back wheels of the vehicle. It fishtailed a moment but then caught traction, and Karl, with one elbow resting out the window and a cold stare in his eyes, aimed the truck right at Lawrence.

"Better jump Larry." advised The Babe, and somehow Lawrence found his legs, leaping onto the frozen river just in the nick of time.

He broke through the ice with a crash and sank slowly to the bottom of the river. When he lay on the bottom, not quite understanding if he was breathing or dying, he saw a small octopus swim up to his face. It studied Lawrence for a moment before skittering off in a jet of ink. Lawrence couldn't see a thing for a moment, but eventually, the ink began to gather and take shape. It was the shape of an old man with a staff.

Chapter Twenty Seven

Robert Bartlett had a hard time falling asleep that night because his mind kept spinning over the bizarre conversation with Helen and Talula from the night before. Now that he had time to think about it, he was ninety-nine percent convinced that it was an elaborate practical joke arranged by his buddies in the archaeological program. Either that, or his aunt's friends weren't playing with a full deck.

He showered in the tiny bathroom and got dressed while his coffee brewed. He ate a Hostess apple cinnamon roll and some leftover crackerjacks for breakfast. And looked for his glasses.

He panicked a little, searching for the thin wire frames that were once his grandmother's. He loved them because they'd been hers, and they looked just like John Lennon's glasses. A few minutes later, he found them underneath his nightstand, stretched them over his face, and took out his wallet. He pulled out his tiny magnet address book and looked for his Aunt Jane's number. He was hoping she could shed some light on who might be behind this prank. As he dialed her number, he began to wonder who even knew about his Aunt in Beaver.

Her phone rang six times, but she didn't answer. Then he remembered his Aunt's secret code to talk, the code he needed to get her to answer the phone. He redialed, let it ring once, and hung up immediately. Then he waited for a moment and dialed again. Aunt Jane picked up on the first ring.

"Hello?"

"Hi, Aunt Jane, it's Bo."

"Oh, I thought it might be you, hon. I guess Helen called you?"

"Yep, she sure did. I actually thought it might be a prank set up by my friends down here. So... is Helen okay? I mean, she had a wild story."

"Oh yeah, she's fine, but she was acting pretty strange when she came over yesterday. What did she want anyway, hon?"

Robert was quick with a response. He really didn't want to get involved in his aunt's affairs with her friends, and now he thought that maybe Helen was a little "cuckoo for Cocoa Puffs."

"Oh, no big deal," he said. "She thinks a girl named Talula who lives up there found some fantastic artifact, but it sounds like it's not anything important."

"Oh yes, Talula, she's a smart cookie, that one. You know she turned down a scholarship at OU to study archeology? Decided to go to Panhandle State to stay near home. Helen said she's studying Chemistry up there."

"Listen, Aunt Jane, I hate to ask, but do you think Helen and Talula are of... sound mind?" He hated the way it came out, but he couldn't think up a better way of saying 'batshit crazy.'

She laughed out loud. "Well, Bo, I can say that they are of sound mind. Why on earth would you ask such a question?"

Robert grimaced at his blunder.

"Poor choice of words, Aunt Jane. I just don't want to drive all that way to look at another arrowhead."

"Well, if you drive all the way out here, you'd better come see me!" she said.

"I won't ever turn down a chance to see my favorite aunt!" he said. "So, how is Uncle Karl?" He remembered Karl from his visits as a kid, but they never really hit it off. Now, Henry was a different story. They had a great time one summer roaming the countryside on Henry's dirt bike. They found arrowheads up on the Beaver River and explored the sand dunes...then it hit Robert:

he remembered the sand dunes and the pedestal. The pedestal with the strange markings on it.

"The same as always," he heard his aunt say. "You know just the same..."

"I'm sorry to hear that," he said. "Well, I have to go, but I think I'll be heading up there soon. Can you give me Helen's number, please?

She did, and he thanked her.

"You better come see me, Bo," Jane said. "You promise?

"I promise. Love you, Aunt Jane."

"Love you, too."

He ended the call with way more questions than answers. The vision of his pre-teen years at his aunt's house had been startling; he could see the pedestal clearly in his mind. Robert decided to take a chance and call his professor, Dr. Wyckoff, to see if he could shed any light on the mystery. With more than a little reservation, he put the black address book back in his wallet and dialed the number of the only man he knew who might have some real answers.

When Helen rose from sleep the next morning, she started through the daily checklist that had been her morning routine for many years. But then she remembered, almost the way you suddenly remember that one of your loved ones is gone. She hadn't experienced that since William left for San Francisco with that peroxide blonde kindergarten teacher, Sandra Kittle. She was a little surprised by how her mind compared the current situation with her past.

William and Helen met in Westfield, Massachusetts, where Helen worked the graveyard shift in a Denny's and used to keep William's coffee cup full.

Helen loved to hear him say, "Thank ya, hon," in his soft Southern accent.

He was kind of old for a college student, probably late twenties, but he had a focus, unlike the other students who sat in booths throwing toast, coffee, and jelly singles at each other.

William was always kind, but as soon as he sat down at his usual table in the back by the fire escape, with his books and study notes, it was all business. Almost every night for six months, he would wear his tweed sport coat that somehow seemed a bit big on his thick six-foot-two-inch frame. With his well-shined brown cowboy boots resting on the rung of the opposite chair and his fiery orange hair, William was quite a sight. Helen averaged about five trips to fill his coffee during the two hours he would sit and study. Then he would pack up his books, put them in his satchel and walk to the cash register to pay his bill, always leaving Helen a dollar tip.

In 1960, at the end of the spring semester, William showed up at the restaurant and asked Helen if he could buy her dinner. When Helen said yes, it sparked a romance between them that was stronger than anything she had ever known. They moved to Oklahoma when he became principal of the Beaver school district in 1963, and they were happy as could be until Helen discovered they weren't able to have children.

It was such a blow for both of them, especially William. He said and did all the right things for many years, but she could tell it was killing him and, therefore, killing them. She started getting the "gonna have to work late tonight" messages every once in a while. Then they became more frequent. Helen wasn't stupid, but she trusted him more than she should have. One day, when she'd had enough and planned to confront William about his late work nights, she came home to find a letter on the kitchen table.

Helen,

There is no way to say this that will be easy on either of us. I am leaving. I am moving to San Francisco. I never wanted to hurt you, but I cannot live like this. I am trying to do the best I can for you financially. My attorney will draft a proposal that allows you to keep the house and the car, and receive a monthly alimony payment. I hope you find the person that you are meant to be with, as I finally have.

William

She cried for a year. She stayed in her house and hid from the world, except for going out once a month to handle her finances. She wished on shooting stars in her backyard, on pennies turned heads up that she found on the ground. She wished for peace in her soul, for magic in her heart, but she found none. And her neighbor Rosa, used to knock on the door twice a week, usually carrying a casserole dish or cookies. Even though Helen ignored the knocking and the doorbell, Rosa kept trying.

One day, Rosa knocked on the door and waited politely for Helen's nonresponse. This time, however, she started talking to Helen through the door.

"Helen, I know you can hear me, and I am not going to go away until you open this door."

Silence.

"Come on, Helen! I made you some fudge, half walnut, and half plain. Let's sit on the porch and eat the whole pan!"

Still nothing

"Alright, Helen, I'm going to sit out here and eat this fudge and talk really loud at you through the door. I'm just letting you know that I am not leaving until you open up the door and talk to me."

Helen scoffed at this ultimatum. She decided to get a soda and turn the TV up really loud. A Ma and Pa Kettle marathon was on, so she turned the volume all the way up. Helen watched three episodes and turned off the TV, confident that she had rid herself of her pesky neighbor.

"I like Ma and Pa Kettle a lot!" She heard from outside the front door. "That last episode is one of MY FAVORITES!!" Rosa screamed. "HAVE YOU SEEN THE ONE WHERE PA…"

Helen ripped the door open with a cigarette hanging from her lips. "What in the living hell are you doing at my door? Can't you take a hint?"

Rosa didn't flinch; she walked right past Helen and into the house.

"Do you want some fudge? I ate almost all the pieces with walnuts, and I figured you would surely eat the plain ones because I know a lot of folks don't like walnuts in their fudge. I sure do, and there are a few with nuts if you prefer those."

Helen couldn't believe this large Osage woman had just waltzed into her house with baked goods, as if it were a Sunday neighborhood get-together.

"Now look here, Missy!" Helen snapped. "You can't come into my house uninvited like that."

"You know my name Helen, it's Rosa, and I brought fudge!"

Rosa held Helen's angry gaze. After a moment, Helen's lip started quivering, and she broke down in a flood of tears, a different kind of tears, the kind that you can cry when you finally know you are not alone in the world. They cried and laughed, made up ugly names for William and his new girlfriend. They talked about the gossip around town, TV shows, books, and movies. They ate all the fudge and came to a couple of conclusions. Neither of them cared if the fudge had nuts or not. If you eat half a pan of fudge, you're going to make yourself sick.

So Rosa brought Helen back into the world, back into some semblance of light and a little bit of hope. Eventually, she started going to the Methodist church with Rosa, or as Helen sometimes called them, the "Swaddlers." She actually liked it better than the Catholic church of her childhood. It was similar in ways but more laid back. Helen met Jane there and became good friends with her as well. Her two new lady friends were there when she found out that William and his new wife had followed a man named Jim Jones to South America, where he and several other people died in a cult-related mass suicide.

All this history flashed back on her in a matter of moments, as she began to sort through the details of her current situation.

"Let's see, we have a half-Cherokee, half-Irish wizard of some sort who has fallen through a portal opened up by a bunch of kids, who are now little wizards themselves. And we have some sort of evil demon that possesses animals and hunts anything magical, that needs to be destroyed before we find a way to help the wizard back to his own land. That pretty well sums it up."

She looked in her closet and pulled out a pair of crisp blue jeans and a brown pearl snap shirt. She pulled her dark, slightly graying hair back in a ponytail and put on her Red Sox hat, a gift from Toby Red Corn, who was a huge baseball fan. Helen looked in the mirror and saw something that had been missing in her for so long: a little bit of hope, a little bit of magic.

Chapter Twenty Eight

Tendigrads rose well before the sun with two main goals for the day: Finish reconstruction of the key to the portal and try to locate the kigatilik. He was very close to fulfilling the first goal, but he had doubts about the octopod's ability to channel the portal's magic. He sensed that the glue he had used wouldn't stand up to that kind of power. He had just put the last piece in when Helen came down the stairs and into the kitchen.

"Good morning, Tendi. Are you a coffee drinker?" She pulled her little-used percolator out of the kitchen cabinets.

Tendigrads looked up from his finished project and smiled.

"I am as of yesterday," he said. "I remember coffee as a child, but I never partook. Yesterday morning, Tommy and Anson introduced me to coffee in your world. I must say it's a truly amazing drink!"

Helen found the coffee maker, placed it on the green Formica counter, and grabbed the Folger's can from the cupboard.

"I hope it's good. I usually have Sanka," she said, popping the plastic lid off the can. "Smells good."

"Indeed, it does." Tendigrads agreed and went back to studying the octopod.

Helen filled the percolator with water, scooped the coffee into the metal basket and plugged it into the wall. Then she joined him at the kitchen table.

"My word, you have it all back together!" she exclaimed.

"Yes, but I'm not sure it will function," he said.

Helen had the same doubts. In truth, she doubted that the piece could be put back together. She thought of Robert, hoping that he might be able to find some answers to help the wizard get back home. As the coffee pot started gurgling, Tommy and Anson shuffled in and sat at the table, sleepy-eyed and yawning until they saw Tendigrads' accomplishment on the table.

"Killer!" Anson proclaimed

Tendigrads was a bit taken aback. "Killer?" he wondered aloud as he looked to Anson.

"Oh, it means really great," the younger man explained. "It's just an expression."

Tendigrads mulled that over and shook his head. He couldn't understand how such an ugly word could mean something good.

"I do not see how our repaired octopod can work. It may be that I am not destined to return to my land. I will address that in time, but for now we must focus our attention on locating and defeating the kigatilik. We must all be clear on this point: The kigatilik is hunting magic, and that includes you, Tommy, and Talula. It will not hesitate to use any creature to hunt us, so I must find and defeat it. "

"We'll help you, Tendi," Tommy assured.

"Yeah, we'll help you!" Anson agreed.

"Help you what?" Talula asked as she strolled into the kitchen, looking more than ready to do anything that needed doing.

The percolator finished its noisy process, and Helen poured a cup for everyone.

"So what kind of help?" Talula asked again. "What's the plan?"

"I will have to deal with the kigatilik alone, friends. I could not ask you to endanger yourselves against this ancient evil."

"Don't worry about it, Tendi. You don't have to ask because we are going to help one way or another," Talula replied rather forcefully. "So it is probably better if you tell us exactly what we should do to best help you."

Everyone looked at her as she took a sip of coffee. "Well, I am just being practical," she said. "If you go off hunting this thing by yourself, then it could find us, and you wouldn't be there to protect us."

Tommy and Anson saw where this was going. They looked at each other with that knowing look of what it was like to debate with Talula Polk.

"I think it would be more practical to try to locate the demon and lure it to a place where I can deal with it, without endangering you and Tommy," Tendigrads said."

"What happens if it decides to go for easier prey like Tommy and me? It makes more sense that it would want to find us first if we were separated from you," Talula studied the wizard. "That way, it could gain more power before attacking you."

At that moment, Tendigrads became acutely aware of the skills of his young apprentice. He held her gaze with an equally unflinching stare until Tommy chimed in with the wizard's own words. "I suggest we let her follow her instincts and support her decision."

To which Anson added, "One of my most important mentors was a young woman who had so much courage and wisdom that men felt threatened by her, and they missed the valuable gifts she could offer. I am grateful I chose not to be so blind."

Tendigrads said nothing, obviously caught off guard that the boys had gotten his goat. He stood up and walked slowly into the living room and back again. He finally sat down at the table.

"It would seem that I underestimated the intelligence or maybe just the inherent stubbornness of my young apprentices," he said. "So let's talk about strategy."

"I'm not stubborn," Talula muttered, to which Tommy spit coffee on his shirt while Anson and Helen fought not to follow his example.

Chapter Twenty Nine

The kigatilik had a difficult time learning Karl's basic functions. When it tried to command Karl to put the bottle down, the challenge was such that it almost lost control. The kigatilik finally decided that a slow reduction in the strange liquid Karl craved would serve best.

Searching Karl's brain for commands on moving the steel wagon was also frustrating. "Keys" could not be found. After a strenuous effort, it determined that "keys" were thrown out in the field in a fit of rage sometime before it entered Karl. A search of the area eventually located keys near one of the strange black metal "oil birds."

After learning the ritual to make "truck" come to life, the steel wagon began lurching around in the field. The kigatilik tried to find a balance of control as Karl screamed for more "whiskey." It relented, and Karl snatched up the bottle, draining the little that was left. Therein lay a glimmer of who Karl Schmidt used to be.

Finally, somewhat stabilized, together the kigatilik and Karl pulled the black truck out onto the road and headed towards the town to find the magic it craved. But Karl insisted on going "home" first to get more whiskey. This enraged the kigatilik, which decided that finding another host was the next urgent objective. Until another host was available, however, it would use Karl.

And so, the truck veered all over the road, as it lurched its way towards "home."

Chapter Thirty

Late on Tuesday afternoon, Don Wyckoff was sitting in his house in Norman, Oklahoma, playing his old Martin D-28 guitar. His knowledge of country and bluegrass music was arguably impressive, as was his expertise in archaeology and anthropology. Don knew a million songs and could belt them out one after another, if requested. When he learned that one of his graduate students, named Robert, played the mandolin, he sought him out after class one day and asked him if he wanted to play some tunes together. Robert was enthusiastic in his response, and the two had become good picking friends over the past three years. It didn't hurt that Don appreciated the quality of the student Robert had grown into under his tutelage, and the two always paused for shop talk between picking tunes.

Don had just set the guitar down, his mind on getting one more cup of coffee, when the phone rang. His wife Ruth answered the wall phone in the kitchen.

"Hello? Oh, hi, Robert. Yes, he's here. Just a moment," she said. "Don, it's Robert!"

"Coming," he said, grabbing his cup. Don put the receiver on his shoulder and bent his head to the left to hold it in place as he poured the coffee.

"Hello, Robert."

"Hi, Dr. Wyckoff, how are you today?"

"Oh, I guess I am doing alright," Don said. "I was just practicing a few of those new tunes. Are you still good for Saturday night?"

"Sure thing, I'm looking forward to it."

"Great, now what can I do for you, son?"

"Well, I was hoping to pick your brain on something," Robert said.

"I don't know how much is left, but go ahead!" Don laughed.

"Some of my Aunt Jane's friends from up in Beaver think they have found an artifact of some kind."

"Oh, one of those..." Don muttered.

"That's exactly what I was thinking, too," Robert said. "But the thing is, there may be something to this. It has to do with the Shaman's Portal up in the sand dunes."

"Shaman's Portal? That already sounds a little questionable."

"Yes, sir, I understand how it sounds, but hear me out."

"Go ahead then."

"There is a pedestal stone sitting in the area of the alleged portal," Robert began.

"Emphasis on alleged!" Don interjected.

"Yes, sir! Well, anyway, I remember when I was a kid, my cousin and I played all over that area. That pedestal stone had an indentation in it that looked like a star with eight arms, and this kid in Beaver recently found a stone octopod in what she claims is an archaeological site."

"A stone octopod... and this kid says it's from a dig site?" Don suddenly sounded more than intrigued.

"Yeah, not exactly a kid. I mean, she is a young adult, and she seems very credible," Robert paused. "But now comes the incredible part."

"Go on," Don said.

"Well, she claims when she placed the octopod on the depression, it fit perfectly... and..."

"And?"

Robert knew he was treading on very thin ice here. This could jeopardize his reputation with the archaeological community at a time when he was beginning to get some recognition.

"She claims it opened the Portal," he heard himself say.

There was silence on the other end.

"Dr. Wyckoff? I know, I know, it sounds crazy," Robert spluttered. "Forget I said anything about it. My apologies."

"Robert, I am going to need you to meet me at Building 9," Don's tone was all business now. "I'll be there in 30 minutes." And he hung up.

"Well, there goes, everything," Robert whispered. He grabbed his keys and wallet, walked out of what was probably going to be his old apartment, and jumped into his two-tone brown Ford pickup to meet his fate at Building 9.

Chapter Thirty One

Jane heard Karl's truck pull into the driveway just as the latest episode of *The Young and The Restless*, her favorite soap opera, was finishing. She got up and went to her room, knowing he would only be staying long enough to get his whiskey. Jane turned on her little bedroom TV and lay down to watch *General Hospital*. She peeked through the curtain to check when he left.

Karl was sitting in the truck, just sitting there staring through the windshield right into the sun. Turning back to the TV, she forgot about him for a minute or two. When she looked out the window again, he was still sitting in the truck. "Must be pretty stone drunk," she huffed under her breath.

Finally, she saw Karl stagger out of the truck. She looked back at her show just in time for the end of the commercial break. "Lemon-fresh Joy cleans down to the shine! What a nice reflection on you!" the television voice trumpeted. She heard him walk by the bedroom and into the storage closet where the cases of whiskey were stored. His boots clopped there and back, and then he was out the front door again. Jane stood up to reclaim her living room, when she heard him come back in.

"Must have forgotten to kiss his wife," she quipped as she stood with her arms folded and stared at the television. She heard his boots again, but then they stopped at her bedroom door. She listened to the doorknob slowly start to turn.

"I'm busy," she yelled.

The door opened, and there was Karl, his shirt covered in vomit and a nasty wound on his neck. He smelled putrid, and his clothes were absolutely filthy. That would have been horrific enough, without the cold, focused look in his eyes and the deer rifle.

"Karl?" she said, her fear rising.

He just stared at her, through her, making her feel like she was an insect. She knew he had finally snapped, and she was going to die.

"Karl, please, don't do this!" she pleaded. Then Karl dropped the rifle and came at her with his mouth open like a wild animal.

Jane's scream was so loud and utterly anguished that Karl paused for just a second; she saw his eyes change. But again he stumbled towards her, grabbed her by the shoulders, and leaned in, mouth open, reeking. She screamed again.

Suddenly he pulled away, stopping only to grab his rifle, and ran out the front door. Jane slumped to the floor, physically unhurt but hyperventilating through her tears. She heard the pickup start, and the spinning wheels shot gravel against her window as it raced out of the driveway. She sat there for a moment, unconsciously touching her amethyst necklace.

Chapter Thirty Two

Tendigrads and his three young apprentices walked in the small grove of trees behind Helen's house, as the clouds gathered to cover the summer sun, offering a bit of a respite from the oppressive Oklahoma Panhandle heat. The wizard led them to a clearing in the middle of the Redbud and Bois d'Arc trees and traced a pattern of glowing, blue smoke in the air.

"U-wo-hi-yu-sv," he enunciated, whipping the wand in the same pattern, repeating the spell he previously had traced in the air. He then turned to Talula and Tommy.

"Belief is a subtle but essential spell for any magic-user; it helps to expand the level of your faith, especially in times of trouble," he said. "Please practice this new spell on each other much as you did with the Laugh spell."

"You got it, Tendi," Tommy said as he quickly began practicing the spell.

"Master Tendigrads, I have a question," Tulula said.

"Of course, ask anything of me."

"Is there any way a spell could go wrong?" she said.

"These initial spells will not work if you are unable to speak the incantation and trace the pattern in rhythm. You cannot harm anyone if you fail, but I appreciate the question and the concern for others, Talula."

She gave the old Wizard one of her rare smiles.

"Good to know." She turned to practice with Tommy.

That's when Tendigrads motioned for Anson to follow him. He led him to a spot within eyesight of Tommy and Talula and started swinging his staff in patterns around his body. The staff became a blur as he accelerated the movements, eyes closed, aiming vicious strikes at imaginary targets from various angles. Finally, Tendigrads stopped the magnificent dance and nonchalantly leaned on his staff.

"I want to teach you how to defend yourself and your companions using the staff, but you will need to be patient," he said. "Learning this rod is very challenging. Anson. I will tell you it is a powerful skill that can be even more important than the ability to use magic."

Anson was shocked by the wizard's speed and grace. Tendigrads' movement through the world was always steady and deliberate, but the dance he'd just witnessed was anything but that. He expected something along the lines of blocking each other like a couple of kids playing with broom handles. Now, he was more than a little worried about his ability to learn the flurry of moves he had just seen Tendigrads perform.

"There are three basic spacings for the two-hand grip: Gadalv Nvya, Ayeli and Asdudi. In English, these Cherokee words mean wide, middle and close. Memorize them immediately." Tendigrads wrote these three words out in the air. "I will demonstrate, and you will imitate my hand spacings while repeating the names. Are you ready?"

"Yeah, I'm ready."

Tendigrads showed Anson the three grips and practiced with him until he had the grips and the Cherokee words memorized.

"Excellent, now please continue to practice while I look in on the others."

He turned and walked back to the clearing where the other two were still practicing their spell. They were absolutely focused on their work, which pleased him greatly.

"Wonderful! I appreciate your commitment. Those wand strokes are really improving, and so is your enunciation," he said as his wand traced the mystical pattern in the air. "Now, we have one more spell to learn today."

"Protection is another spell that, when cast correctly, will show very little evidence of success but can offer defense against shadow magic as well as other dark powers. You should enunciate the syllables in short, strong bursts, 'a-da-s-de-lv-di'!" He shouted as he traced out the pattern again towards Tommy.

"I definitely felt that!" Tommy exclaimed.

"Good, remember, it must be clear and strong. Now practice!" He returned to check on Anson.

"Gadalv Nvya, Ayeli and Asdudi!" Anson uttered as he moved through the three grips with his staff.

"You have learned those grips in a very timely fashion, Anson," the old master noted. He walked to the words hanging in the air and, with a wave of his wand, they disappeared.

"You will now learn the four stances that will be the basis of all your moves, so it is imperative that you learn these extremely well before you learn any strikes."

Once again, he wrote the four positions in the air and added stick figure diagrams to show the positions. "'Achuffa tuklo, tochina, ushta,' these are the four positions you will learn; these are simply the numbers one to four in Choctaw. Now practice well."

Tendigrads spent the next hour moving back and forth, working with his apprentices. At the end of their training session, he was confident that Talula and Tommy could cast the six basic spells of Laugh, Cure, Belief, Protection, Safety and Sleep, and that Anson had mastered five critical strike and defense patterns. He was amazed at how well and how quickly these young people learned.

As they were going back inside, they heard a siren wailing somewhere to the north. It froze Tendigrads in his tracks, "Great Spirit!" he exclaimed.

"It's okay, Tendi. It's just a police siren," Anson said. The wizard sat still and listened to the fading wail.

"What an unsettling sound," he muttered as he caught up with the others.

Chapter Thirty Three

Before there was a Don G. Wyckoff, Ph.D., there was a teenager named Don, who helped build grain elevators throughout Kansas. These concrete towers were typically the first thing you saw when driving between the tiny towns of the Kansas plains. One of these fantastic concrete monoliths that Don had worked on was in the city of Phillipsburg, Kansas. To call Phillipsburg a city is much like calling a house cat a dangerous predator. Technically, Phillipsburg was a small town with an estimated population of just over 2,000. The addition of a grain elevator was a giant event for Phillipsburg and the surrounding area. Of course, the townspeople were so proud that they held a huge celebration featuring a weekend of music, square dancing and pie-eating contests.

The oldest residence of Phillipsburg was a strange old woman named Mary Choslo, or Glove Lady as the people of the town called her, who lived in the middle of town. Looking at Mary, you would have no doubt she was the oldest person. And she had amazing stories to tell about the town's development. She claimed to be the wife of Captain John Shaw, who had been the commander of Fort Bissel. The rumors about Mary were as old as the town itself. Some said she was a showgirl from Chicago, or a Pawnee woman who killed her Pawnee husband and escaped to live with the whites in Phillipsburg. Others suggested she was a Creole voodoo woman with strange powers of suggestion and illusion, the latter being the talk of the most imaginative minds in town.

Mary always wore gloves; in fact, she had an extensive collection of them in all styles and colors. This afternoon she was wearing a set of red opera-length velvet gloves with tiny white beads embroidered in the shape of a wing on each hand. Her dress was horribly torn and dirty, and she also wore a pair of dungarees under the dress and a badly discolored man's suit coat. Her hat was a weathered, black flat bill made of felt that appeared to be too big for her tiny head. It was hard to tell by looking if she was indeed Native American, Mexican, or possibly Asian. She was so old her face had deep crags. But her eyes, those fierce unnerving eyes, one brownish black, and the other hazel were clear and alert as a sea captain in a squall.

At two of the picnic tables near the bandstand sat the young men who had labored so hard to build the town's monumental new grain elevator. Mary walked right up to the tables and looked each man up and down. As she strolled around the picnic tables, she finally stopped behind young Don Wyckoff.

"You, come with me," she uttered. The other men stared at Mary Gloves and began to laugh at Don.

"You better go with her, Donnie!" one of them said.

Don Wyckoff had been raised to give respect to his elders. Even though he really wanted nothing to do with this crazy old woman he had seen walking around the grain elevator the past few months, he rose from the table and followed the old woman.

"What can I do for you, ma'am?" Don asked politely as they stopped about twenty feet away from the picnic tables.

"I hear tell you gonna be a, uh what you call 'em uh, archaeologist?" she whispered.

"I am going to college this fall, and yes, I am going to study archaeology. How did you know that?"

"I know more than most folks thinks I know, and I think some archaeological folk oughta have this thing I know about. It's old magic, real old. I think you better take it with you when you go to school."

Don was just trying to bide his time and be kind to the crazy old woman, but he was puzzled by how she knew about his school plans.

"What's your name, ma'am?"

"Mary Choslo, kind of you to ask."

"I'm Don. It's nice to meet you." It just went against Don's grain to have a conversation without proper introductions. "How do you know about me going to school?"

"Those boys you work with talk loud, Don," she said, showing a toothless smile. "I heard 'em up at the diner talking about you." She pulled out a dirty red bandana wrapped around something and handed it to Don.

"I been carrying that fo' along time, and I know you gonna figure out what to do with it."

Don took it from her hand and slowly unwrapped the heavy object. He had never seen anything quite like it before.

"Where did you get this, Mary?" Don asked, examining the object. When she didn't answer, he looked up, but she was gone. He quickly looked around; she was nowhere to be found.

"There is no way that old woman could have moved that fast," Don muttered to himself as he jogged towards downtown, looking for her. "She couldn't have just disappeared." But he couldn't find her anywhere. Eventually, Don gave up and put Mary's gift of an odd-shaped stone wrapped in a bandana under the seat of his Hudson pickup truck and went back to the festival.

When he got back to the picnic tables, all of his work crew had gone back to their rooms except his foreman, Edgar Manson.

"Where did you get off to Donnie? What did the crazy lady want?"

"Oh, she thought I was her nephew, and it took some convincing to show her that she was mistaken," Don lied. "I didn't want to be mean to her, so I took a little time to talk with her."

"You have a good heart, son. I've seen her around town. She's harmless, I hear, but she is a little 'touched' from what folks say."

"Yes sir, I would agree with that."

"I was just waiting on you to get back, making sure no harm came."

"Thanks, Mr. Manson," Don said. "I am going to head back to my room and get an early start on the road tomorrow. Gotta get back home to say goodbye to my family before I head for New Mexico."

"You did good work for us this summer, Donnie. You have fun digging up rocks or whatever it is you archaeologists do." Mr. Manson gave him a vigorous handshake and said goodbye.

Now, some 40 years later, Dr. Don Wyckoff sat in his pickup truck in front of Building 9, sifting through the gossamer of these memories. He remembered telling that story to one of his instructors at the University of New Mexico. After showing the stone to a well-known expert in Southwestern archaeology, the man harrumphed loudly and told Don, "You won't last long in this field if you are going to be so gullible." He walked off, leaving Don holding his artifact in the hallway of the archaeology department.

He was stirred from his memory by Robert's brown Ford pickup pulling up next to him in the parking lot. The two men opened their respective doors and closed them almost simultaneously.

"Follow me, Robert," Don said. Robert did just that, trudging behind like a man who was just about to have his dog put down. They got to the door, and Robert slipped the key in the lock and jiggled it as he pulled up on the handle. He let go of the knob, and the old white door with the big plate glass slowly opened on its own accord.

"Don't even know why we lock it," Don muttered, walking briskly into the former barracks. "Alright, Robert, I will need your help with this next part; hope your back is good."

Robert's dread began to recede a little. Dr. Wyckoff didn't seem angry, but something odd was happening.

"Sure thing, Dr. Wyckoff!" Robert eagerly responded.

Don walked to the back of the building, ducking his head to peer between two-by-four racks full of bins that stored dinosaur bones, rocks, fossils, old wagon wheels, taxidermy species, and antique iron tools with a surprisingly high level of organization.

"We need to move this old buckboard frame out of the way, and it's going to be heavy," Don said.

They pushed the massive oak relic out of the way until there was a small gap that Don could squeeze behind the buckboard. He worked his way back through the maze of antiquities, occasionally exclaiming as he bumped his head or shoulders.

Robert could hear him progressing through the artifacts, and eventually, he heard Don scraping away at something.

"There it is!" he exclaimed. One minute he seemed far away, the next he appeared in front of Robert, on his knees from behind the buckboard. He handed Robert a metal box and stood up to brush the dust off his jeans. To his surprise, Robert saw that the box was actually a battered old Howdy Doody metal lunchbox, scuffed up and tied together with an old leather belt.

Don took the box and walked back to the front of the building, motioning to Robert to follow him. He sat at the old desk where, over the years, dozens of students had carved their names in the walnut veneer. Robert sat down across from his former professor, and the real storytelling began.

As he unwound the old belt from around the lunchbox, Don told him about how he came by the still-unseen object.

"I was in my second year when I showed this to my first professor, and, of course, he told me in no uncertain terms that I was an idiot," he said. "So, I hid it away, and when I came to Oklahoma, I decided to keep it here in Building 9. I felt there was something special about it, but I had completely forgotten about it until you told me your story."

He handed the box to Robert and motioned for him to open it. Robert sat it on the desk and flipped the one rusty clasp that remained on the old lunchbox. He lifted the gingham-wrapped item out of the box and removed the cloth. The stone octopod was exactly like the one that Talula had described to him on the phone.

"Oh my god, Don! Uh, Dr. Wyckoff. What do you think this means?"

"I am not at all sure, but I think we better get to the bottom of it."

"Well, I guess since we are coming clean on all this, I should let you know the rest of what they told me," Robert said.

"Holding out on me?" Don raised an eyebrow. "Spill it, then. I'm all ears."

"Yes, sir. They claim that when the portal opened, an old Cherokee man came through and is in Beaver with them right now," Robert said. "Apparently, the octopod was damaged, and the old man is stuck in this world."

"Tell that story to anyone else I know, and it would get you a one-way ticket to the funny farm!" Don said. "But I believe you, so let's go."

"To Beaver?" Robert asked.

"Yes, I'll call Ruth. You drive."

Chapter Thirty Four

When Lawrence finally awoke, he was lying in a hospital bed with an IV in his arm, the steady beat of his heart rate amplified by the machines monitoring him. His bizarre dreams had finally subsided; he could barely remember something about Babe Ruth and Roger Maris.

He tried to talk, but his throat was so dry that he could only croak; however, his throat noise was enough to get the nurse's attention. She was in his room in a split second.

"I'm right here, Mr. Carr. Just take it easy now. You've been through a rough row!"

"Water, could I get some water, please?" he whispered.

"Of course, just a moment!" She poured him some water, scooped up ice chips in another cup and set them on his table. She raised the bed so that Lawrence could easily reach the table. Nurse White was an old pro. She quickly took his vitals, notified the doctor, and began to answer Lawrence's many questions.

"Well, it was a coyote bite that somehow caused a very toxic reaction in you."

More pieces of the dream came back. He remembered the coyote and how it turned into...something, but he just couldn't remember what.

"I don't remember driving. How did I get here?"

"Mack and Harlan Whitaker happened to be driving behind you when your car ran off the road. They pulled you out of the car and brought you here. I don't think you would have made it if they hadn't seen you."

"I don't even remember getting in my car, but I do remember that coyote. He was just sitting there by my car, staring at me," Lawrence said slowly. "Then when I turned, the bastard snuck up and bit my ankle. That's all I remember until I woke up here."

"How are you feeling now?"

"Well, I don't feel too bad at all, just exhausted and hungry. Is there any chance of getting some food? I think I could eat a horse!"

"I'm sure we can get something better than that," she replied. "Oh, Helen, from your restaurant, came to see you."

"Oh no! Maxine's. How soon can I get out of here and back to work?"

"Mr. Carr, you can't go anywhere for a while," Nurse White said. "The doctor needs to check you out, and you don't need to worry about Maxine's right now. Helen is handling things."

He tried to get up but was so woozy he couldn't get his legs out of the bed.

"Rest, Mr. Carr. I'll get you some lunch, and the doctor will check on you in just a minute."

"Yeah, rest sounds good." Lawrence closed his eyes.

He was suddenly very tired; his adrenaline rush was more than his exhausted body could stand.

He wondered about his dream but couldn't put the pieces together, not yet anyway.

Chapter Thirty Five

The kigatilik had no knowledge of kryptonite, but when Karl had reached for Jane's throat, the powerful stone hanging from her neck caused a burning that had ripped through the demon. "Kryptonite" was the word that Karl had used to describe the stone. It had thought to switch hosts again to Jane, but the kryptonite had prevented that. Now, it could sense that the first human host kigatilik tried to enter after Coyote had possessed this same stone as protection. It seemed that it would have to stay in Karl until the magic user could be found. Perhaps the magic user possessed no such protection. It had a surprise for the wizard's wand fire. This time, the demon would be ready.

The kigatilik would need to hide for now, and Karl knew where to go. So Karl drove with the truck full of whiskey and bullets, heading north out of Beaver, just minutes before the county sheriff received Jane's 911 call. The demon had learned to heed the warnings of its host, and Karl was telling it to flee from something called the police. It also knew the only way for the magic user to return was through the thin place between these two worlds. That is where it would lie in wait. The kigatilik was so very hungry for the magic, and this world had very little, but the magician would sate its hunger very soon.

Chapter Thirty Six

When Sheriff Jesse Baxter got the call about Karl Schmidt, his first thought was, "We all knew that would happen eventually." Thankfully, Karl hadn't killed Jane, but that didn't make him any less dangerous. He flew down the road, lights flashing and siren screaming, which was very unusual for Beaver, Oklahoma.

Jesse thought about Henry Schmidt. The two had been in the same grade and good friends. They both were on the high school baseball team; Jesse played first base, and Henry pitched. They spent more than a few nights hanging out, drinking illegally obtained Lone Star beer, and talking about what they were going to do when they graduated. They both wanted to join the Army, and they made a pact to do just that. Henry joined up in October, and two months later, they were at his funeral.

The town reeled from the senseless loss of one of their own. Henry's parents, Karl and Jane, went through their grief in opposite ways. Karl turned into a zombie and had to be led around by friends at the service, while Jane was a mess of unbridled tears and anger. She found it impossible not to lash out at everyone and everything, but when it came to her husband, she wouldn't acknowledge his existence. They buried Henry with winter wind and Jane's mournful cries howling around them. The bitter temperature and unsettling sorrow cut through the very bones of the folks of Beaver. For Jane, it was like Karl was dead too. It was not a scene Jesse could ever erase from his mind.

When it came time to enlist, he was torn about what he should do. He wanted to honor the pact that he and Henry had made, but his friend's death weighed on his decision. His dad finally talked him into joining the Air Force, and he was glad he did. Jesse spent his four years as a military police officer, or MP, in Seoul, South Korea, where he threw young airmen into the drunk tank or broke up their fights. After getting out of the Air Force, he returned home to help his dad with the farm. But when old Barney Mangum stepped down as the sheriff of Beaver, he ran for the position and won.

Jesse pulled into the Schmidt's gravel drive. Jane, who was sitting on the front porch in her bathrobe and house shoes, stood up and moved towards his car. Jesse grabbed his hat, exited the car, and pulled his service revolver out of its holster.

"He's already gone, Jesse," Helen said in a sad, shaken voice.

"Is he driving his truck?

"Yes."

"Are you okay?"

Helen shrugged and shook her head. Jesse went back to his car and radioed an alert for Karl's truck, announcing that the suspect was considered armed and dangerous. He then returned to Jane, who had resumed her place on the porch.

"I better look inside, Mrs. Schmidt." She just waved her hand towards the house as if to say, do whatever you want.

Jesse checked the house, revolver drawn, not really expecting to find anything but just following procedure. When he emerged to question Jane, he saw that she had a cigarette in one hand and was silently sobbing. Jesse sat down beside her and put an arm around her shoulder. She leaned against him and had a long-overdue cry.

"Tell me what happened, Mrs. Schmidt," he said. She told him the whole story, venturing off into more than a few tirades about Karl's drinking.

"Karl was so strange when he came into the bedroom. He didn't say anything to me; he just looked like some sort of animal. Then he reached for my neck and backed up, screaming," she said. "It wasn't a natural sound. Then he grabbed his rifle and high-tailed it out of here."

"He took his gun?'

"Yes, and a whole bunch of shells and whiskey, too."

"Mrs. Schmidt, please go somewhere else until we find him. Do you have somewhere you can stay?"

"I'll figure something out." She patted his knee and forced a smile.

"I can take you somewhere, or you could wait at my office until you figure it out. Shoot, you could stay with Teresa and me..."

"No, Jesse, I can stay with Helen Clayton. Give me a second to throw some clothes on, then can you just drop me at her place. Is that okay?"

"Of course, Mrs. Schmidt."

"Please try not to harm him. He is still Henry's daddy." Once again, she burst into tears.

Chapter Thirty Seven

"Humility is the ability to honestly see your strengths and your weaknesses, and to have the willingness to work on those weaknesses." Tendigrads remembered the words of Aayia DeWilde, his first mentor in all things of nature and magic. He thought of her often, especially given his current situation with these three young people who had fallen under his tutelage.

The dire situation with the demon who had followed him into this world also reminded him of his honored mentor and her demise at the hands of a creature like that. He thought back to the last discussion he had with Aayia, right before she'd gone tracking a group of Yunwi Tsunsdi, or "little people," who had suddenly turned evil and were hunting magic users.

Aayia had thought it extremely unusual that the Yunwi Tsunsdi had turned violent and dangerous. Their natural behavior was to stay hidden. At their best, they were known to offer aid to the First People; even at their worst, they were not cold-blooded killers.

"I have heard legends of dark creatures in the far Northern lands of perpetual ice that feed on the spirits of magical beings. I wonder if such a creature has possessed the Yunwi Tsunsdi," Aayia had said. "I can't think of another reason; I am going to investigate the situation. When I return, we will discuss a strategy for dealing with this threat."

She ignored a young Tendigrad's plea to accompany her, stating that she would do this alone. But the next morning, he could sense Aayia's magnificent staff calling to him for help, so he gathered a group of her apprentices and tracked her down in a clearing, her life force mortally wounded. Something had stripped her magic powers. Her green staff had been shattered in combat, and she was lying in the grass beneath a rock ledge. There was no sign of her attackers. When she saw her apprentices, she forced a smile.

"Tendi, you need to know this. I was right about the Yunwi Tsunsdi being possessed." She spoke with great difficulty as Tendigrads knelt beside her with tear-filled eyes.

"No tears. There's no time for tears," she admonished. "This creature feeds on magic. Thankfully, I believe I have defeated it. Fire is the key to fighting this creature. I chose poorly when it attacked me. I tried to block the psychic attack with magical defense, and it drained my magic so quickly that I fell unconscious for a moment. Then it tried to possess me. I was close to succumbing, but I remembered who I was long enough to cast fire, and it died screaming in my head. Unfortunately, much of my own life force died with it. I am broken beyond repair."

"No! No! We are going to heal you right now."

Her apprentices had already begun casting all forms of healing, cure, protection and prayer spells. But Aayia was fading.

"You cannot heal what I no longer have, my loved ones," she said, closing her eyes. "Tendi, take the crystal from my staff and build another one for someone deserving." As she slipped out of the world, the wind sang a lonesome wailing sound, and birds halted their songs.

It was a sorrowful memory for the old wizard, but his mentor's experiences would be most valuable in the coming struggle. Tendi knew that he could not leave this world until he was positive the kigatilik was defeated. He wasn't sure he would be able to go back through the portal at all. He needed a clue as to where the shadow beast might be, and the only person who might be able to help him was the man who had encountered the creature. The man named Lawrence. As Tendigrads walked back to Helen's house with the others, he announced his intentions.

"I need to speak with your friend Lawrence as soon as possible. Can we go back to the hospital?"

"Of course, I hope that he is awake, but we can head over there right now," Talula offered.

"Yes, we need to go there quickly," Tendigrads said. "Lawrence is the last one to come into contact with the kigatilik. He might offer some clues."

"Should we all go?" Anson asked.

"We will all stay together until this creature is defeated. It will hunt us because it has no choice. If it cannot find magic to devour, it will eventually fade away," Tendigrads said. "But it can still feed on any common life force for some time, and many of your community could perish before that happens."

Helen was sitting on the back porch steps when the group reached the house.

"There are some roast beef sandwiches on the table in a Tupperware container," she said. "Better get them before they get soggy."

"Let's take them for the road," Tommy suggested.

"Where are you going?" Helen said.

"We need to go to the hospital and talk to Lawrence," Tendigrads answered.

"Oh, should I come too?"

"Of course, Helen."

"Let's take my car," Talula said. "It's so hot! I could use a little air conditioning!"

Helen retrieved the sandwiches and sodas, and they all climbed in Talula's car, where they devoured the food in short order. Even the stoic wizard made gracious "mmmm" sounds as he wolfed down a sandwich. When they got to Lawrence's room, he was awake and eating a bowl of chicken soup with some crackers and a Sprite. His face lit up as his kitchen crew came into the room. He didn't notice Tendigrads at first.

"Hey Mr. Carr, looks like you are feeling a lot better than the last time we saw you," Tommy said.

"We were worried for you, Lawrence, but you do indeed look better," Helen added.

"It's good to see y'all." He leaned back in his bed and set the spoon back in the bowl. "I don't know what that coyote had, but it sure did a number on me."

"Lawrence, this is Mr. Tendigrads," Talula said. "He was hoping to ask you some questions about that coyote. He is...with the wildlife division of Oklahoma."

"You can call me Tendi, Lawrence. I'm glad you are feeling better."

"I'd be glad to help," Lawrence said. "But there's not much I can say, other than the coyote was acting strange when I first saw it, sitting by my car, not growling or scared at all. I knew something was weird, so I went back in to get my gun. When I turned my back, I guess it just slipped up behind me and took a bite out of my ankle. I don't remember anything after that."

"Did you have any dreams?" Tendigrads asked casually, holding the other man's gaze.

Lawrence stared back and closed his eyes. As if in a trance, he recited the dream to Tendigrads in specific detail. The others stared in wonder as Lawrence, in a monotone voice, relayed his encounter with the two baseball legends, the coyote, the spider, Karl Schmidt, and, of course, the octopus. Once he finished, Lawrence slowly opened his eyes and adjusted himself in the bed, looking around the room, confused.

"Sorry folks, I must have nodded off there. I don't remember any dreams," he said. "I am kinda tired, though, so I think I'll catch a few winks. Oh, Helen, please put a sign up at Maxine's saying 'Closed until Further Notice.' We'll open as soon as I get my legs back under me. Don't worry about your pay; I'll make sure you're all taken care of." And he was out instantly.

"Well, remind me not to have any dreams around you, Mr. Tendigrads!" Helen commented with a hint of worry in her voice.

"Who is Karl, and where can we find him?" Tendi asked.

"Karl is married to my friend, Jane Schmidt. Oh, do you think he is in danger?" Helen said. "And what about Jane? We need to get to her now!"

"I agree."

They once again climbed into the Maverick while Helen filled in Tendigrads on the Schmidt family's tragic history.

Chapter Thirty Eight

Robert and Don wasted very little time getting on the road, just time enough for Don to call Ruth and explain briefly why he was blazing off into the wilds of Oklahoma on another archaeological excursion. While Don was taking care of his business, Robert called Helen and his Aunt Jane, but neither answered. He drove the truck down the block to J Botie's Quick Stop and filled his truck with gas.

He went into the little shop to get some snacks for the road, hoping that the attractive Native American girl was working this afternoon. As luck would have it, she was there. When he opened the door and set the bells on the handle jingling, she graced him with a warm smile.

"Hi, Robert," she said.

"Hi, Carol!" he said, trying to hide his nervous excitement. She made him feel so awkward that he felt he would trip on thin air in front of her.

He went to the Hostess Bakery rack and grabbed packs of random donuts, fried pies, cinnamon rolls and Zingers, then went up to the counter to pay. Carol looked at the pile of sugary snacks with a rueful grin as he poured a couple of large coffees to go.

"Robert, are you okay? Does your mom know how poorly you are eating?" she said. "I mean, I could maybe make you some real food if you need it!"

"My professor, Don, and I have to book it up to the Panhandle, and we are kind of in a hurry, so this will probably be lunch and dinner." He thought quickly and added, "Not that I would turn down a home-cooked meal! I mean... I don't mean to say you were asking to cook me a meal, and I would sure eat anything you cooked, uhh..."

She was enjoying his bashfulness, drinking in his rugged good looks, when suddenly the lid on the cup of coffee he was holding popped off and splashed all over his hands and boots.

"Son of a b.... oh, I am so sorry, Carol! Sorry to cuss!"

"Oh my gosh! Is your hand burned? I'll get some ice." She said, grabbing a cup from the soda machine and slipping it under the ice dispenser.

"I'm okay. Sorry about your floor! Have you got a mop? I'll clean this up."

"I got it! Don't worry. Let's see your hand." She gently took his hand in hers to inspect it. She poured some ice into a clean towel and placed it on his hand.

"Keep that on your hand for a few minutes. Hopefully, it won't blister."

"I'm so clumsy. Really sorry about that, Carol."

"Shhh, You can make it up to me sometime."

"Sure, you name it," he said.

"Great! You can take me out to dinner, and we'll call it even!" She went to the backroom to get the mop.

"Sure," Robert grinned, sounding a little more excited than he had planned.

Carol was trying not to laugh out loud. She really liked Robert, but it was clear he might never ask her out, so it was up to her to make the first move.

That's when Don Wyckoff rushed in the door.

"Come on, Robert! We gotta hoof it!"

Robert gathered up his snacks and coffee and headed for the door.

"I'll call you Carol!" He waved and was gone.

Carol chuckled to herself as the door slammed shut.

"Kinda hard to do if you don't have my number there, Robert," she muttered. "Hey, don't worry about paying for the baked goods, coffee and gas! It's on me this time!"

She looked out the window as the two archaeological adventurers climbed into the truck and headed out to Interstate 35.

Chapter Thirty Nine

Jane should have called Helen, but given the day's events, who could blame her? When Sheriff Baxter asked if Helen was home, she replied, "Oh sure, there's her car."

She went to the front door and knocked. Then she knocked again and peered through the window, but no answer came. She didn't want to sit on the front porch and was terrified that Karl would show up. Jane wished she'd checked to see if her friend was here before she let Sheriff Baxter drive away.

She went to the backyard and sat down on the edge of a rusted steel lawn chair under the shade of a magnificent pecan tree. It felt so strange being out in the world after hiding in her house for so long. She already missed her television shows, and of course, her Valium, which was starting to wear off. She reached into her purse and realized that she had forgotten to bring her prescription.

"Oh God, Oh God!" She dug frantically in her purse searching for the pill bottle. She finally dumped the whole thing on her lap. Jane was not prone to obscenities, but the string of sentence enhancers she screamed into the hot Oklahoma air would have made a sailor blush.

She flung her purse towards the house and sagged down into the chair, weeping uncontrollably. All of her emotions came crashing down: Karl's descent into alcoholism, her withdrawal into her own falsely calm world and, of course, the loss of Henry.

Henry was all she and Karl had lived for, but Karl had filled Henry's head with all those war stories. That was what had taken Henry from them. It was Karl's fault. Well, it seemed to be his fault, and she'd made it clear to her husband whose fault it was. Maybe he had done everything he was capable of doing to repair their relationship, but she had shot him down every time. Eventually, he had given up himself – and the bottle took him.

Jane cried till she had no tears left in her body. She had no idea how long she'd been sitting there when Helen came around the corner and touched her shoulder. Jane jumped up so fast that she nearly crashed heads with her friend. When she saw it was Helen, she grabbed her in a desperate embrace and somehow found more tears to shed.

Helen held her as she sobbed. But when Jane saw the three young people accompanied by an older gentleman walking towards them, she gathered herself, smoothed out her dress and attempted to feign normalcy.

"Hello, Tommy, Anson... and is it Talula?"

"Yes, how are you, Mrs. Schmidt?" Talula said.

"Hi, Mrs. Schmidt," Tommy and Anson said in unison.

Jane looked warily at the old gentleman for a moment before Helen introduced him.

"Jane, this is Ebrnt Tendigrads, Tommy's great uncle from Rosa's side of the family. Ebrnt, this is my dear friend, Jane Schmidt." She grabbed Jane's hand as she looked into Jane's eyes, trying to support her friend as she spoke.

Jane offered Tendigrads her hand and said, "Pleased to meet you, Mr. Tendigrads."

"'Tendi' is what my friends know me as. It is indeed a pleasure, Jane."

"Let's get inside out of this heat, dear. We just got back from your place!" Helen said, leading her friend towards the house. Jane stopped and looked at her.

"Was Karl there?" she asked anxiously.

"No, what in the world is going on?" Helen said.

"Well, something terrible has happened," she said as they walked up the steps to Helen's back door.

Tommy bounded ahead of the two women and held the door open.

"Something has happened to Karl. He tried to attack me with his bare hands like he was some kind of animal."

"Oh my word!" Helen exclaimed. "Are you alright? Did you call Baxter?"

"Yes, they're looking for Karl right now. I don't know what got into him. He has never been like that with me. We have had some shouting matches, but he never laid a hand on me," Jane shuddered. "It was just so horrible and strange, Helen. It was almost like he wanted to bite me! When his hands touched my neck, he screamed like a wounded animal, grabbed his gun, and ran away."

"I lost my medicine," she murmured and began crying again. Helen looked at Tendi.

"You are among friends, Jane. We are all here to help you." Tendigrads' calm, soothing voice was reassuring. Even though she had just met this man, Jane somehow believed for a moment that things would be okay.

"It looks like you could use some rest, Jane," Tendigrads said. He traced a small pattern in the air and whispered the sleep spell. Jane didn't even notice, she started yawning, and her eyelids were drooping.

"Yes, sleep, that would be good," she murmured.

Helen led her to the bedroom and returned with a nod of thanks to the old wizard.

"She takes those damn pills like candy. You can see what happens when she doesn't have them," Helen announced.

Tommy's face tightened as he recalled his mom's desperate need to be free of her addiction, a fight she eventually lost. "I would have given anything to have helped my mom," he said.

Everyone in the room became quiet. Tommy never spoke of his mother's death, and he regretted letting the sentence come to his lips. Tendigrads looked at Tommy with compassion.

"Maybe you could tell me what happened with your mother?" he asked. But Tommy was already walking outside.

Helen filled Tendigrads in on Tommy's history, including his mother's overdose on pain pills. The wizard's eyes teared up in empathy for this young man.

"He has a quiet courage, and he is blessed with great friends," he said. "Thank you for telling me, Helen."

He went out to the patio, where Tommy sat slumped down in a chair.

"Tommy, I think we can help Jane," Tendigrads said. "What I mean to say is we can offer her some aid, but eventually, the choice will lie with her. I will need your help."

"I can't stand to see this happen again." Tommy choked out. "Just take all the damn pills and pitch 'em in the damn ocean for all I care!"

"Yes. It seems that some things have gone wrong with the medicines of this world. But we can help her together. Come with me."

Tommy rose slowly from the chair and followed the old wizard back inside. While Jane slept, Tendigrads, Tommy, and Talula stood by her bedside and offered spells of Cure, Bless, Aid and Prayer to help alleviate the worst of Jane's physical and emotional dependencies on the drug. When it was over, it was Tommy's turn to break down.

"I hope it does some good," Tommy cried.

Then the old man held Tommy while all of those years of pent-up hurt poured out of him.

When they returned to the living room, Tendigrads asked Helen if there was any way to know where Karl might be.

"Not exactly. He often hangs out on his land just off Route 23," Helen said. "Other than that, he could be anywhere in his truck. I'll call Sheriff Baxter and let him know Jane is here. Maybe he could tell me more. They may have caught him by now."

"I hope for their sakes they haven't. I am convinced the kigatilik has possessed Karl," Tendigrads said. "If he is caught, I don't know how the sheriff will protect himself."

Helen thought for a moment. "Let's start with calling the sheriff. If we could get through, we might be able to warn him. I doubt he would believe us, but maybe we could convince him Karl is much more dangerous than he thinks."

"That would be a start. We should wait here until we hear from the sheriff or Jane's nephew. Although I fear that they may not truly believe our predicament."

The old wizard looked tired as he moved to the couch. He stretched out his lanky frame, propped his head on one end, his feet on the other, and was soon deep in thought. Helen couldn't help but think he looked like he carried the weight of the world on his shoulders. Talula, Tommy, and Anson slipped outside and stretched out in the patio chairs under the pecan tree. They sat for a while until Tommy broke the silence.

"This is all just too much to believe. I mean, am I ever going to wake up from this dream? There is some sort of evil, magic-drinking monster running around our town, and an old Indian man fell out of a portal, taught us how to do magic, and is probably stuck here in our world. Oh, and we just now temporarily healed a lady who was addicted to pills by waving sticks around in the air and speaking Cherokee."

"Yeah, if someone had told me that last week, I would have called the funny farm to take them away," Talula agreed.

"Oh, I dig, it's like *The Lord of the Rings* in Oklahoma," Anson said. "But you have to admit, Tommy, it's pretty sweet having magic powers."

Tommy looked up, and it was clear that he was barely holding back tears.

"Yeah, pretty sweet... It would have been even sweeter if I could have had magic powers before my mom and dad died." He hung his head to hide his face. Talula went to him, put her arms around his neck, and didn't say anything. She just waited till she felt him slightly move away from her, and then sat back down in her chair. Anson was also watering up.

"I really hate these chairs," Anson said, standing up.

"Why on earth do you hate the chairs, ATV?" Talula asked.

"Well, it seems like every time someone sits in one, they start bawling like a baby."

Talula stood up and slugged Anson semi-playfully on the shoulder and shot back. "Oh! You clown!"

Even Tommy broke into a grin. He was impressed by Anson's ability to break the tension with humor, especially at times like these, when it was so desperately needed.

Chapter Forty

Robert pulled over in Woodward at the DX station to get gas and tried calling Aunt Jane and her friend, Helen, again from a pay phone. Dr. Wyckoff pumped gas and complained about having to pay eighty cents a gallon.

"It's highway robbery," he complained loudly. "It was sixty cents in Norman. Who do they think they are?"

Robert had no luck with his aunt, but Helen picked up his second call. "Hello?"

"Hello, Mrs. Easton. It's Robert Bartlett."

"Oh, Robert! I am so glad you called. Jane is at my house now," Helen said. "She has had quite a scare, I'm afraid, but she's resting at my house and will be just fine."

"What happened? I tried to call her twice today and got no answer."

Helen hesitated because she really did not want to get too deep in his family's business, so she gave him the light version.

"She and Karl got into a big fight, and she is staying with me for a while."

"Did Karl hurt her in any way?" She could hear the concern mixed with anger in his voice.

"She's fine. She doesn't have a mark on her." Helen left it at that, hoping he would not press the issue until he could talk to Jane personally.

"Is she asleep?"

"Yes, but I will have her call you as soon as she wakes up. Is that okay, hon?"

"Well, I will be there in about an hour and a half."

"That's wonderful!" Helen said. "She will be so glad to see you."

"It will be good to see her, too," Robert said. "But the real reason I'm coming is that I might have something to help your friends. Give me your address, and I'll be there as soon as I can."

"I'm at 201 East 9th right on the corner of 9th and Quinn, down the street from the bowling alley, on the right."

Robert wrote the address down on the back of his hand.

"We'll see you in about an hour and a half."

He hung up and checked the coin slot for loose change, but found none. Don had gassed up the truck and had two cups of coffee and two bags of M & M's waiting as they headed into the setting sun on the last leg of their trip to the Panhandle.

Chapter Forty One

Sheriff Jesse Baxter had one clue concerning Karl Schmidt's whereabouts, but considering that Karl was armed, drunk, and bat shit crazy, he would need back up before he went waltzing up to the old cabin on the Schmidt homestead.

Jesse radioed his buddy Eddie Scroggins and asked him to meet up on Route 23 at the entrance to Karl's oilfield at two o'clock that afternoon.

"Yeah, Karl Schmidt may have finally gone off the deep end. He attacked Jane and then drove off in his truck, fully loaded for bear," Jesse said.

"Shit fire! Is Jane okay?"

"Physically, she is fine, but well, you know."

"Be there in ten."

Jesse sat in his patrol car, waiting for Eddie to show up and ran through his checklist. He had alerted the state police and even gone so far as to warn the Feds. If Karl fled to Kansas or Texas, that would be federal jurisdiction, and he would be their problem. Jesse mulled over his plan to get Karl out of the cabin without anyone getting killed.

Eddie pulled up next to Jesse in his brand-new Oklahoma Highway Patrol cruiser. He rolled the window down with a big wide grin.

"Damn, Eddie! That is one hell of a ride you got there!"

"Just got it on Friday! AC all day, kid! It's gonna make me soft!"

"Looks like a beast! Got a 440 in it?"

"Yep, 440 with the 727 TorqueFlite tranny and a 9.25-inch differential!" Eddie said. "Kid, it will haul ass!"

Eddie always called Jesse "Kid." To be fair, he called everybody younger than himself, "Kid." At twenty-six years old, Eddie was only two years older than Jesse. They had become friends over the past couple of years while working together on cases.

"Wanna follow me?" Jesse asked.

"Lead on!"

Their cars crossed the old cattle guard and rattled up the dirt road that led past the pumpjacks on Karl's land. The cabin came into sight once they were past the oil field. This was where Karl had grown up. He had started renovating it before Henry died, but now it lay in total disrepair. As they got closer, they saw that Karl's truck was not there, and the cabin door was open, hanging on by two screws on one hinge.

Jesse got out of the car, hand on his revolver. "Hey, Mr. Schmidt, you in there? It's Jesse Baxter. I just need to talk for a minute, sir."

No answer. Jesse shook his head. Eddie had been covering him from behind the door of his cruiser. He now moved up to the front of the house on one side of the open door. Jesse held it open and glanced inside before entering the shack. They quickly secured the two rooms of the cabin and began looking for any clues.

Jesse holstered his revolver and pulled his flashlight from his belt. As he panned it around the main room in the cabin, he froze.

"Holy Hell!!"

Eddie quickly turned towards Jesse and gasped in horror when he saw the gory sight of a coyote nailed to the wall with its front paws sticking straight up in the air as if to say, "I surrender." Its eyes had been removed and had been tied by their optic nerve to the pads of its paws. Both eyes seemed to be alive; they appeared to move just slightly.

Eddie pulled his gun in an instinctive reaction and shot, blowing the abomination and the wall out into the heat of the Oklahoma sun.

"What in God's name was that?" Jesse yelled.

"Hellfire, I don't know! Karl is into some screwed up sort of taxidermy."

Suddenly, Jesse remembered the incident with Lawrence Carr and the coyote bite. And the description from Mack and Harlan Whitaker of a coyote chasing Carr's Lincoln and attacking the vehicle as it rolled down the road.

"Let's have another look at that thing."

"Think it's going to look any better since I shot it?" Eddie asked.

They went outside to view the mangled carcass. One eye lay in the dirt, covered in sand. The other was still attached to a paw. But it looked dry and dead, no hint of life like they'd seen in the cabin a few minutes earlier.

"It must have been the light shining on it somehow, but I could have sworn those eyes looked alive in the cabin," Eddie said, trying to convince himself that his own eyes had played tricks on him.

"I saw it too, Eddie," Jesse said. "Maybe it was just the light, but I would have sworn they shifted to me when I looked at them."

"I don't know, sounds crazy," Eddie agreed. "But one thing's for sure: Karl isn't here, so I guess we struck out. When you write the report, you gonna leave out the part about the moving eyes?"

"Yeah, I think I'll skip that part," Jesse grimaced.

The two lawmen checked out the rest of the cabin before leaving in their separate cars, each replaying in their heads the vision of the mutilated coyote and its searching eyes.

Chapter Forty Two

The sand dunes that fill the area north of Beaver cover about five hundred acres in the Oklahoma Panhandle. Known as "Little Sahara," these natural phenomena are wondrous and strange, to say the least. It was no accident that Karl and the kigatilik came to terms with each other in that remote, desolate place.

The kigatilik had never possessed a host with such intellectual ability and willpower. Trying to break Karl had proved impossible. However, by tapping into the Karl's mind, the demon was able to learn a different technique: compromise.

Karl craved power and respect, and his dependency on whiskey wasn't helping him with these goals. Indeed, Karl had lost friends and stature in the community because of his addiction, and self-loathing drove him to need more and more whiskey.

By the same token, the kigatilik understood that Karl had skills that past hosts lacked. He had the metal wagon, the fire stick, and an overwhelming knowledge of this world that would take ages for the demon to incorporate into its own memory. So the two entities agreed to co-exist, in essence becoming one as Karl, a decision that seemed to lift Karl's spirits. The kigatilik, after all, cared little for names.

Karl knew the legend of the Shaman's Portal and the magic that supposedly existed in the sand dunes. When they walked further among the dunes, they could feel the magic radiating through the sand. Together they learned, becoming more powerful in the wellspring of seemingly infinite magic. It turned out that Karl was also a dark entity, which made for a more perfect union. It was his idea to find the coyote and create a horrible, beautiful totem as a message for anyone who came looking for him.

Karl could see the two lawmen through the coyote's reanimated eyes, could see them shake with fear, and he loved it. Now, with his pickup truck hidden in the dunes of Little Sahara, Karl was drinking his rationed portion of whiskey a little less every hour. The need for whiskey was slowly slipping away. According to their agreement, the pain began to recede as well. When Karl's mind began to clear, he could focus on hunting the wizard; he could kill the wizard and survive in this world with the newly discovered magic. Karl had learned that revenge was one of the sweetest experiences a being could know, and the ki-gatilik was starting to have its own desire for these feelings. Together, they began to visualize everything they could do to the old magician.

Chapter Forty Three

Robert pulled into Helen's driveway at 7:30 pm with Don slumped against the passenger door, fast asleep.

"We're here, Doc," Robert announced. Don popped up, his grey hair slightly ruffled, piercing blue eyes set to full intensity.

"Right," he said, as if he had not just been asleep. He grabbed the lunchbox and joined Robert as they walked up to the front door.

Helen had been looking out the window and quickly opened the door for the two archaeologists.

"Welcome, gentlemen. How was your trip?"

"Long," Don said, extending his hand. "Don Wyckoff."

"Thank you for coming, Dr. Wyckoff," Helen said. "I'm Helen Easton."

"I wouldn't have missed it for the world," he said and looked around the house.

"South Boston?" Don ventured.

"Yes, that's right," Helen replied.

"Great town. I used to get up that way in the summers."

Just then, Jane emerged from the bedroom. When she saw Robert, a smile lit up her face in a way Helen hadn't seen in quite some time. "Bo!" Jane hugged her nephew. A head taller than his aunt, he picked her up and hugged her back.

"Are you okay, Aunt Jane?" he said. "If Karl hurt you, I want to know."

"I am truly better than I have been in quite a while, Robert," she said. "It feels like a heavy load has been lifted from me."

Helen could see the difference. Jane's skin looked vibrant, and her eyes were alive with hope. What wondrous magic this man who came from the Shaman's Portal had brought to help her friend!

"Aunt Jane, this is Dr. Wyckoff," Robert replied.

"Please call me Don. It's my pleasure, Jane," he said, taking her hand in both of his.

"So, where is this artifact?" Don asked, eager to get past the introductions and into the matters at hand.

"It's on the kitchen table." Helen gestured to the kitchen, and they all followed. Don sat down at the table, staring in wonder at the reconstructed stone octopod. Although the pieces seemed to be well connected, there were still some fragments missing. The artifact seemed somehow lifeless. It was hard to explain, but it just felt broken.

"Hmmm, let's see here." He opened the lunchbox and pulled out the cloth-wrapped object. Removing the cloth, he revealed what looked like an exact duplicate of the fractured octopod. He set it down on the table, and it felt like the air in the room changed. Both artifacts were the same size, shape, color, and except for the cracks, looked identical. But the octopod Don and Robert had brought from the university was alive with energy.

"They look the same to me," Helen said.

"I believe you are mostly correct, Mrs. Easton." Don agreed.

"What are those things?" Jane asked.

"According to your friend here, they may be the key to another plane of existence," Don responded nonchalantly.

"I doubt very seriously Helen believes that sort of poppycock!" Jane snorted, looking to Helen for confirmation. Her friend did not meet her gaze. Jane looked to Dr. Wyckoff, who wore a hint of an all-knowing grin, and then to Robert, whom she knew she could trust.

"I think it's about to get even weirder, Aunt Jane," Robert said, as the man in the pearl-snap shirt and the John Deere hat walked in the back door with three young people.

When Tendigrads saw the duplicate octopod on the table, he raised his eyes to the ceiling and said something in Cherokee, "Osda!"

Then he looked at the two men he assumed had come to offer him aid.

"Wado." Tendigrads said as he bowed to them.

"It means 'Thank You,'" Talula said.

"I deduced that, young lady," Don remarked, which immediately got a rise from her.

"Oh well, sorry for questioning your amazing skills of deduction," she shot back.

Don gave a hint of a smile, impressed by this brave young woman with a sharp mind.

"My apologies," Don said. "It's Talula, if I remember correctly." She quickly stuck out her hand to shake with Dr. Wyckoff.

"That's right, it's Talula, and my apologies as well," she said. "I read your publication earlier this summer, *Secondary Forest Succession Following Abandonment of Mesa Verde.*"

"Was someone punishing you by making you read that?" he laughed.

"Not at all, but I did have some questions about..."

"Dr. Wyckoff, Robert, my name is Ebrnt Tendigrads," Tendi interjected. "This is Anson Vernon, Tommy Red Corn and, of course, Talula Polk."

"Nice to meet you both," Anson offered.

"Yeah, we appreciate the help," Tommy said.

"Just as I am the reason you are here, Miss Polk is the reason I am here." Tendigrads explained.

There were many questions and not nearly enough time to answer them all. Jane was skeptical of the idea of magic and portals, but as the evening unfolded, she understood they were speaking the truth. And she became suddenly very concerned for Karl.

Of course, the two archaeologists had to see a few parlor tricks as Talula and Tommy cast the Laugh spell on Dr. Wyckoff a few times. Each time Don sat silently, grinding his teeth, before he burst into laughter. He shared his story of how he came by the other octopod, a story Tendigrads found deeply intriguing.

"So much mystery. What an amazing puzzle life is!" Tendi said. "As I see it, we must draw the kigatilik into the portal when it opens. And we don't know if merely placing the octopod on the pedestal will open the portal or not."

"Do you remember what time the portal opened, Talula?" Robert asked.

"Yes, it was close to one-thirty in the afternoon. I don't know exactly, but I'm pretty sure that was within fifteen minutes."

"Well, as you say, Master Tendigrads, it might not open at all, or it might open when we set the key in the pedestal," Robert said.

"I believe that High Sun and Dark Night might be the best times for the portal to open. If my ciphering is correct, the one-thirty in your time reference is very close to High Sun."

"What do you mean by High Sun, Tendi?" asked Anson.

"We call it solar noon in our world," Don answered.

"When the sun is closest to us," Robert added.

"Oh," Anson said, wishing he'd paid closer attention in science class.

"That well could be it," Don agreed. If that is the case then Dark Night might be the next time the portal opens."

"But we will have to deal with the demon. It has to go back with me through the portal, and if the portal does not open, we will need to destroy it," Tendigrads said. "We cannot allow it to survive in your world."

"But it's Karl!" Jane cried out.

Poor Jane Schmidt. These people were planning to get rid of this... monster, which was also her husband. He was a mean, verbally abusive son of a bitch, but he was her husband, and she didn't want him to die. "Are you saying there is no hope for Karl? Are you saying this monster thing has already taken him?"

Realizing his callousness, Tendigrads looked at Jane.

"Unfortunately, that is the most likely scenario," he said. "But if there is a way to save Karl, you have my word on the name of The Great Spirit that I will do it. I do not offer false hope, as honesty is the only true path to honor. If he can be saved, we will do it."

Jane sat quietly for a moment before she found a few more tears to shed.

Chapter Forty Four

While there were many unknown factors, the group developed a range of possible plans, including an emergency evacuation strategy. Even so, Tendigrads was reasonably certain of a couple of things. The magical folk needed to stay together because the kigatilik would try to drain each of their magic if they became separated. The other certainty was that Tendigrads would be its primary target. The young apprentices possessed barely enough power to combat such a creature, but they could offer supporting magic. Anson would stand with the magic user to provide physical defense employing his own staff's enhancements. Tendigrads hoped that it wouldn't come to that.

Helen would stay with Jane at the house where she could comfort her friend, who was coming to understand that her husband might be gone for good. The two archaeologists would oversee the placement of the key in the receptacle. The group would arrive at fifteen minutes to dark night, at which point, the portal would hopefully open, and the kigatilik would chase Tendigrads through it. Then they would all go to KFC the next day and drink Coca-Cola in honor of their wizard friend.

However, if the demon refused to take the bait, Tendigrads would attempt to kill it again. It would take some time to confirm that it was actually gone. Then there was the unthinkable. What if Tendigrads couldn't defeat the demon? What if it had figured out how to defeat Tendigrads? Then these young people he had grown to love would be doomed.

A plan was set for the young ones to escape in Anson's Plymouth with the archaeologists doing the same in Robert's truck. They were to head straight to the sheriff and try their damnedest to explain the situation. If Tendigrads failed, it would be up to the people of this world to destroy the kigatilik.

Tendigrads and his three apprentices discussed these scenarios as they drove in Anson's car to the portal. Of course, Talula, Tommy and Anson were not on board with the whole "run away" if the other plans failed. They objected vehemently, but Tendigrads wouldn't budge.

"You will do as I say in this matter, Talula!" he ordered.

It surprised none of them, that Talula was leading the dissent, but she finally folded her arms over her chest and muttered, "Fine!"

Robert and Don were doing much the same, throwing around a few hypotheses about what was happening here in the name of time and space. Robert touched the amethyst that Jane and Helen had given him.

"Strange that this little piece of amethyst is supposed to protect us against this thing," he said.

"Yes, but I think this whole day goes way beyond the 'kind-of-strange' category," Don agreed.

They arrived at the portal site twenty minutes ahead of dark night. The place had an eerie feel to it; even if you lived near there and visited the sand dunes at night, it felt different somehow, rife with mystery.

They parked their vehicles and set out on foot to the sight. Tendigrads became wary, sensing the shadow magic. He also sensed something else, something very old that felt much like the power of his world. He was trying to understand how this magic was suddenly so strong. His first thought was that the people of his land had somehow discovered the portal and entered looking for him, but he decided it was highly unlikely that someone else had found the portal. His second thought was more sinister. What if the demon had found a different source of magic here? What if he was feeding off that source? The magic he felt coming from the sand dunes surrounding the portal was strong. If the demon had tapped into this mysterious source, Tendigrads' courageous group might not stand a chance.

"We are close," he announced and stopped walking. He nodded to Talula and Tommy, and they began casting a simple set of protective wards on themselves and the rest of the group. As they continued, Tendigrads wracked his brain trying to think of alternatives to facing a more powerful foe than anticipated. They made their way to the pedestal site and felt a cool breeze. It was the first cool air they'd felt in more than three months.

"The pedestal is right here," Talula said, pointing it out to Don and Robert. Don illuminated the pedestal with his flashlight and saw the indentation on the rocks. "Well, I'll be!" he exclaimed.

Tendigrads' anxiety was breaking his focus. He realized the demon was already at work, using some form of fear spell on the old Wizard. He muttered a quick incantation, "To-hi-u-s-di" and moved the head of his staff as he spoke each syllable. Most of the anxiety drained away. At the same time, he felt the demon's angry energy as he broke its spell.

"It's just like I remembered," Robert said. "Should we give it a try?"

Tendigrads nodded slowly, scanning the area around them. Robert set the octopod that Don had hidden away for decades into the grooves of the pedestal. It fit perfectly. The cold breeze and the wind became stronger.

"How long until dark night?" Tendigrads asked.

"Three minutes," Don answered.

"Talula, did the wind pick up like this when you opened the portal the first time?

"No, I mean, I certainly wasn't aware of it, but it..."

Her answer was interrupted by an explosion that came from the area where they parked their cars.

It was so loud that they all dropped to the ground. A few seconds later, a hub cap from Anson's Road Runner came tumbling out of the sky and landed about five feet from Talula.

They were all in shock. Even Tendigrads was stunned, though he quickly assessed that he had been correct about the demon's growing power. The wind increased to a wail, and the temperature dropped so unnaturally fast that they all began shivering. That snapped Tendigrads out of his stupor.

"Everyone crowd around the pedestal!" he commanded and started tracing a pattern in the air above the portal.

"U TLI U GA NA WA!" he shouted, and the air around them became much warmer. "We will stay next to the pedestal," he shouted again. He was sure the strange wind was the kigatilik's magic. He recognized the fire spell as one he cast on the demon in their previous battle.

Suddenly a flash of purple light shot straight at the group. It appeared to have no effect until Talula started screaming. The amethyst stone had morphed into a nasty-looking purple spider on her necklace that she swatted away from her neck. The others saw purple legs begin to wiggle from their amethyst necklaces as the kigatilik systematically destroyed all their escape routes and defensive charms.

Tendigrads knew that something was not at all in balance here. He thought perhaps the beast enlisted the aid of some darker force to fight for it. These spells were beyond this creature's intellectual ability to understand, or they should have been.

"U-DA-YV-LA-DV A-LI-S-DE-LV-DO-DI!" he shouted a protection from shadow magic spell as he whipped his staff through the air with stunning speed.

As he finished the spell, something flashed out of the corner of his eye, something rushing to attack him. He had no time to cast another spell before the grim face of Karl Schmidt was staring him in the eyes, nose to nose, unflinching.

"Are ya afraid of me, old boy?" Karl asked in a mocking tone, slowly tilting his head back and forth. His grin was pure malice, and as he raised a finger, the wind spinning around the group increased with tornadic speed.

Tendigrads was frightened, more frightened beyond anything he had ever known.

"You and I are not of this world! We must return to our own!" Tendigrads screamed. Behind him, the wizard felt the magic of the portal starting to hum.

"Oh, not yet 'Ole Hoss!' We gonna have some fun here, me and you and these little morsels. Then maybe I'll take you back to our world, and we can have some fun there!"

"Uncle Karl! What are you doing? You got to fight against this thing!" Robert shouted.

Karl turned and saw his nephew, but he wasn't deterred. A second later, Karl grabbed Talula by the hair.

"Robert! Always doing the right thing, ain't ya boy." He yanked Talula's hair up to expose her neck.

"Doing the right thing ain't all it's cracked up to be," Karl sneered. "I'm proof enough of that. Now it's time for some fun!! This little miss is gonna taste good!"

As the portal began to roar, Talula screamed in horror. Karl closed his eyes and drank in her fear with malicious pleasure. Talula was usually more than capable of taking care of herself, the bravest of the brave, always in control of every situation. But not this one.

The fear and despair in Talula's scream awoke something in Anson. He loved Talula with everything in his soul, and he had learned a long time ago that she was her own person who did not need to be protected from schoolyard bullies, a point she'd made clear to him on several occasions. So when Anson made his move, he really didn't try to calculate where this surge of heroism came from. It might have been the spells that were cast on his behalf; it might have been his minimal training from Master Tendigrads, or it might have been the love he had for his friend. Regardless, he struck with a brutal strength and speed that surprised even himself, cracking the staff against the back of Karl's skull with a sickening sound. For a brief minute, Karl was stunned. As soon as Tendigrads saw Anson's move, he knew the fight was on.

The staff Anson struck Karl with burst into flames, and Karl was on the young man's neck in an instant.

"NV-YA TSU-NA-LA-SI-DE-NA!" Tendigrads shouted as Karl sank his teeth into brave young Anson Thomas Vernon. Karl looked down as vines erupted from the ground and wrapped around his legs. He ripped the massive vines into shreds and stumbled away from Anson, who fell to the ground like a sack of potatoes. Talula screamed, and Tommy rushed to the aid of his fallen friend.

"What a weak little Stone Feet spell. I'll keep it on file, 'Ole Hoss!' I'm thirsty for you, and I believe I'll have me a drink," Karl hissed.

The sky changed; the opening portal made the air warmer. Then the portal's green light exploded as Karl leaped at the Cherokee wizard as Tendigrads bared his neck in an invitation to feast. Then Karl ripped into his flesh. Tommy and Talula shouted in horror as Ebrnt Tendigrads leaned back and welcomed Karl into his embrace. Just as suddenly, the green light was gone, the cold and wind began to recede, and the Shaman's Portal swallowed Tendigrads and the kigatilik, sending them out of the Oklahoma we know and back into their own world.

Chapter Forty Five

It just so happened that Sheriff Baxter was driving north on Highway 23 that night to check on Karl's cabin again when he saw the explosion. He gunned it for the sand dunes and ran up in time to see Tendigrads and Karl disappear through the portal. He picked up Anson and carried him to the car with Tommy and Talula on his heels. They got into the police cruiser and rushed to the hospital. Baxter was trying to come to grips with what he had seen, even as Tommy and Talula cast every spell they could to help Anson.

"I think he's gone!" Talula cried out desperately.

Tommy finally responded to Baxter's questions. "Yes, Sheriff, you saw what just happened, right?"

"Hell, son, I don't know what I saw. This day takes the cake for the craziest of my life."

"We'll explain what we know about it, but first get us to the hospital fast. Can you call Helen Easton and ask her to go pick up the two archaeologists? You're going to want to talk to them, too."

"Alright, we'll do it your way." Jesse grabbed the radio and told the station to call Helen.

Talula was beside herself. "Tendi's gone, too. That thing was on his neck!"

Tommy put his arm around her as they sped towards Beaver.

"Why was it so cold out there?" Jesse asked.

"Magic," Tommy said.

When they got Anson to the hospital, the doctor insisted they remain in the waiting room. After a heated argument, they were allowed to stay.

Once he examined Anson, the doctor looked very worried. "This looks like the same thing that happened to Lawrence Carr," he said.

Sheriff Baxter's response was a clipped, "Yep."

They hooked Anson up to a respirator and cleaned the wound, but his fever spiked so badly they weren't sure what to do. The doctor and nurses packed bags of ice around him, but nothing helped. When Talula and Tommy started chanting Cherokee and waving their wands around in the air, the doctor shook his head.

"I honestly don't know what more to do for your friend," he said. "I am sorry. We will make him as comfortable as possible, and maybe by some miracle, he will snap out of it. Mr. Carr found his way back. Perhaps your friend will, too."

And then it hit Talula; she could almost see the patterns Tendi traced when he healed Mr. Carr. "I need a Cherokee dictionary, and I need it now!" she said.

"Where are we going to get that?" Tommy replied.

"I don't know, but we need that or someone who speaks Cherokee."

"Old Cypher Jones lives pretty close by, and he speaks Cherokee," Sheriff Baxter said. "But it's late. He may be asleep."

"This is important! We need him! Would you please get him now!"

"I'm on it," Baxter said and left the room.

A few minutes later, Helen and Jane arrived, accompanied by Don and Robert, who carried Anson's charred staff.

Once again, they were intercepted, this time by a young nurse, but the doctor just waved her away. "It's okay, Lori, let them in."

Tommy filled the others in on what had happened, and then he noticed, with relief, that Don had the lunchbox. Don saw Tommy's eyes move towards it and patted it to reassure the young man that he had the octopod. As they waited, Talula sang songs to Anson and told him they would get him fixed up real soon.

"I believe Anson saved your life, Talula, most likely all of our lives," Don offered. "If he hadn't struck that thing and given Tendigrads that split-second to cast a spell, I think that monster would have killed us all."

Talula wept, nodding vigorously.

It wasn't long before Sheriff Baxter appeared with an old Cherokee man, who looked more than a little sleepy.

"Osiyo," Talula offered as she bowed slightly to the new-comer.

The man responded in English, in a disgruntled manner, "Why are you taking me from my bed at this hour?"

"My apologies, sir, but I need you to teach me the words for 'cure,' 'shadow,' and 'poison' in Cherokee."

" I can do that, but who do you think that you are, a medicine woman?"

"I am," Talula stated.

"But you don't know the language," he said.

"My language is very limited," she said. "Unless you help me learn these words, my friend will die."

"I have only heard of shadow poison in the oldest legends of our people. How do you know this to be shadow poison?

"Because he was bitten by a shadow beast, and every moment we spend talking, his life force is being eaten away by that poison," she said. "Now, will you teach me the words?" Talula was trying to be respectful, but she knew the old man didn't believe her.

"Anvwodi Udayvladv Adahihi," Cypher Jones finally uttered.

"Anvwodi Udayvladv Adahihi," Talula repeated carefully.

"That is very good."

She kept repeating the phrase as she began to trace the patterns in the air with her wand. She could see Tendigrads' hand moving through the air as she tried to copy the patterns that were just barely in her mind's eye. She said the syllables slowly and eventually, it was like Tendi was guiding her hand as she repeated the pattern. Suddenly, the crystal in Anson's staff began to glow, and the designs and her syllables locked into perfect synchronization. Then she passed out, nearly hitting the floor as Tommy and Helen broke her fall.

She was only out about thirty seconds, but in that time, Anson's vitals had started to stabilize, and his fever was dropping. The people in the room breathed a collective sigh of relief. Talula opened her eyes and stood up.

"You did it, Ta! You did it!" Tommy shouted as he lifted her and swung her around.

"Truly a miracle! Praise God!" Jane cried.

"Indeed!" Dr. Wyckoff concurred.

Anson's doctor came through the door to see what all the noise was about and was shocked to see the young man's vitals returning to normal. After conducting a thorough exam, he turned to everyone, amazed. "By all accounts, this boy should be dead. What happened in here?"

"He just got better," Talula said.

"We prayed for him!" Jane said.

"Yes, truly a miracle, " Cypher Jones winked at Talula.

"Do you think you might give the boy some rest now?" The doctor was now taking charge.

"Of course Doc, thanks for saving him," Sheriff Baxter said.

"You know damn well I didn't have anything to do with it, but I think he will pull through now, almost exactly like Lawrence Carr."

As the group exited the hospital, Sheriff Baxter threw his hands up in the air as if to stop everyone from going anywhere. "Alright, let's all head down to the station. I'm going to have to hear this whole thing from front to back."

"I tell you what, Jesse, why don't you just come over to the house, and we will give you the whole story over there. I've got coffee and food, and I don't want to be stuck in your tiny office till 6 in the morning," Helen offered. "What do you say?"

"Sure, that sounds good. Who needs a lift?"

Tommy raised his hand in acknowledgment. "I bet Talula will ride with us, too."

They looked at Talula, who was deep in conversation with Cypher Jones. They gave each other a big hug, and Talula skipped to the patrol car.

"What was that all about?" Tommy asked.

"Oh, Mr. Jones has agreed to teach us Cherokee."

"We! Wow, Talula, are you ever going get out of my business?" Tommy smiled.

"Probably not, Tommy. If I ever saw someone who needed help getting their business in order, it's you," she laughed.

"Oh, here we go. I can't believe I have gotten this far in life without your specific guidance. You know I am a grown person, right?"

"Oh, you're welcome and don't worry, I'll always be there to set you straight. We need you, Tommy. No need to thank me."

"Jeez, you are just unbelievable..."

The unlikely friends continued their bickering until Sheriff Baxter turned on the radio to KOMA as a Uriah Heep song whispered out of the speakers.

"He was the Wizard of a thousand Kings.

And I chanced to meet him one night wandering."

Just like that, they stopped bickering. Instead, they sat next to each other in the back of Sheriff Baxter's cruiser, listening to this serendipitous gift and remembering their dear friend and mentor.

THE END

Epilogue

Nearly two years passed in Beaver, Oklahoma, but the town still wasn't quite the same. Dr. Wyckoff convinced Governor David Boren to close the park and begin excavation of the site near the Shaman's Portal. The project was to be headed by Robert Bartlett, with many visits by Dr. Wyckoff.

They uncovered an amazing pre-Clovis site that changed the way historians around the world perceived early cultures. They built an amazing resource center that became a University of Oklahoma-Panhandle campus for the young men and women working on the site. One of those young women was none other than Talula Polk, who, at the insistence of Dr. Wyckoff, became Robert's apprentice and right-hand person at the Center.

Jane offered the land use for the Center on the old Schmidt Cabin site, and the Center was named The Henry Schmidt Center for Archaeological Resources. Helen and Jane were dedicated volunteers at the Center and were rarely seen one without the other.

A month passed before Anson was completely healed. Once he was back to full strength, he developed an interest in martial arts, in particular, working with a Bo staff. Once a week, he drove to Liberal, Kansas with Talula to study with a grand master. He even entered a few tournaments, which he won handily. Anson and Talula were another pair that were rarely seen apart.

Tommy was often with them when he was in town. He had become quite the bookworm, devoting time to studying the history of the First People, especially that of the Cherokee and his own people, the Osage. He and Talula also spent many hours at the house of Cypher Jones learning the Cherokee language.

But most of the time, Tommy was on a Greyhound bus to Tahlequah, Anadarko or Durant, searching for answers that might give him hope of seeing his mentor again.

There was talk of opening the portal annually on that same day at solar noon for five minutes. Those who knew most about the portal proposed leading an expedition through the portal, in hopes of finding news about Tendigrads, but that idea was quashed. That left nothing to do but wait, which they did. And still do. They wait and hope that the portal might someday offer clues about what happened to their friend and mentor, Ebrnt Tendigrads.

Acknowledgments

I feel incredibly fortunate to have the support of my family, friends, and creative community throughout this long journey. Their energy and encouragement have been invaluable, and I am deeply grateful to each of you. There are a few special people I'd like to acknowledge. Brian Eads, my longtime music collaborator and dear friend, has played a crucial role in helping edit and refine this book. Kreta Dawn generously took the time to provide critical feedback and uplifting encouragement. Christina Adams handled the bulk of the editing with great dedication. Finally, my wife Becky deserves my heartfelt thanks for the countless hours and immense effort she invested in pushing this story to its final conclusion. I truly could not have done this without all of you.

Gregg Standridge

About the Author

Gregg Standridge has created all his life. Writer of songs and composer of music. Digital designer and artistic wood marquetry carpenter. Award-winning Choctaw artist. Shaman's Portal is his debut novel, although perhaps the Wizard Tendigrads has frequented Medieval Faires with magical wands and original stories that now come together. Perhaps you've seen him?